Queen of the City 3

The Life of a Female Rapper

An Urban Hood Romance

Tamicka Higgins

© 2015

Disclaimer

This is a work of fiction. Names, places, characters and events are all fictitious for the reader's pleasure. Any similarities to real people, places, events, living or dead are all coincidental.

This book contains sexually explicit content that is intended for ADULTS ONLY (+18).

Chapter 1

I got out of the car and followed her up to the second floor of the apartment complex. I could smell the marijuana smoke as soon as I began walking up the stairs and it completely engulfed me when we walked through the door. Through the thick smoke, I saw lighters firing up more blunts and the silhouettes of various women standing around, watching me as I walked in. "Follow me," Quandra said as we walked through the sea of women straight to the back room. She knocked twice and opened the door. She sat on the bed with a blunt hanging out of her mouth. She blew a cloud of smoke into the air as soon as I walked into the room behind Quandra. Her lips were covered in red, eyebrows arched to perfection. I could see her eyelashes extending out far beyond her eyelids, resembling mosquito legs. Her eyes were sky blue and her peach-colored skin seemed to have been painted onto her body with perfection. On the top of her head, long red hair flowed down like a sensuous fire. She stood up to me as I leaned against the dresser.

"So, you're Lyric, huh?"

"Yeah."

She smiled, "Quandra told me a lot about you. A lot of good shit," she looked to my side, glancing down at my ass, "yeah, you thick as a bitch, too."

If I closed my eyes, there was nothing in this world that would have convinced me that she was a white girl. She had the attitude and characteristics of a black woman. She walked over to the window, her ass jiggling effortlessly inside of her gray yoga pants. Just then, two more girls walked in behind me, "Malley, we got one of the niggas down for tomorrow. We workin' on the other two, though." She inhaled another drag of the blunt as she turned around, "Cool. Make sure all five of them niggas are down, otherwise, ain't shit movin." They both turned and left the room as Malley passed the blunt to me. I grabbed it from her hand and inhaled it, allowing the weed to sit in my lungs for a few moments before I blew it back out. I didn't cough once as I passed it back to her, "That was some G shit," she said, smiling in approval of how I just handled the blunt, "not even coughing once? Aight, Miss Lyric. Well, like I said, Quandra told me a lot about you, and I think you'd be perfect here, you know what I'm sayin? You got the looks for it and from what I hear, yo' ass is as hard as they come," she leaned towards me, whispering in my ear, "you're the perfect fucking killer."

She winked at me and walked back to her bed, taking another hit of her blunt. I had no idea what the fuck was going on here. I didn't know if this was a prostitution ring or what but it was something about Malley that I liked. It was her assertiveness, the way she seemed to run whatever shit she had going on here. It was in that position of power that I saw for myself. Her cute smile seemed to get lost in the thick smoke as Quandra leaned on the dresser right beside me. I looked to the right out the window and for a moment, I saw Big Mama's face outlined in the smoke. *That weed must be hitting quick*, I thought to myself as I refocused my eyes in that direction. A tear fell from her eye just as Quandra walked into her, dispersing the vision that I had. She went over to Malley, "So, what you want me to do with her?" she asked as Malley looked right at me. Malley smiled, "Don't do nothing. This is perfect for her, and she doesn't need convincing either, I can tell. She's not going anywhere."

Soon after that, Quandra walked out of the room and left us alone. Malley leaned back on her bed, "So, let's talk," she said, her crescent smile barely visible through the smoke.

"Talk about what?"

"About how we can be mutually beneficial for each other."

"I'm listening."

I took a seat next to her as she passed the blunt back to me and explained what they had going on. It was an all-female stick-up operation. They set up stripping events for groups of niggas in the city, and when they put their guards down, they robbed them blind. It reminded me of what I did to Big Tuck a while back, except I went in to kill. The way Malley was talking, killing them wasn't something that they wanted to do. They just wanted the money, and they made a few hits in one city before they moved to the next. It really had been a flawless operation for them because honestly, what nigga wouldn't fall for a fine ass stripper with his pants nearly off his legs. I guess they found the key weakness in most of the dudes in the world—pussy. Sometimes they fucked them, at times they made like they were going to and then pulled the pistols out. Either way, they got what they wanted and left.

Malley was the head of the slick ass operation. They called her Hot Tomalley because of the color of her hair and her attitude, but it eventually got shortened to just Malley. From the looks of it, she was a bad ass white girl that didn't have a fear of anyone or anything. Immediately, I was drawn to her and the way things were going, I felt she thought of me the same way. She scooted up to the edge of the bed and positioned herself right next to me as she rubbed her hand on my thigh and passed the blunt back to me. I glanced down at her hand, inhaling the marijuana and letting it rest in my lungs before I blew it out. She was a freak, but honestly I didn't expect anything different. I'm pretty sure every chick in this little clique fucked with each other in one way or the other.

"So, you down or what?"

I inhaled once again, "I'll fuck with y'all for a minute, you know what I'm sayin', just to see what y'all on."

She took the blunt from me and inhaled,

"Aight, that's cool. Well look, if you up for it, we runnin' a spot tomorrow night. One of the girls ran into some off brand niggas at the strip club the other night. She said they had bread, though, so we want to see what they are on. Just show up here tomorrow around 10 pm. Oh, and make sure you are wearing something to show off that phat ass of yours. I saw that shit from the front as soon as you came in."

I took another hit of the blunt and passed it back to her as I stood up, "Aight."

I felt her eyes scanning me as I left the dark room and stepped into the hallway. Quandra was in the front room sipping on a drink in a red cup when I came out. A few other girls were scattered throughout the room, watching my every move as I walked towards Quandra.

"So, what's up? You down or what?"

"Yeah. I'ma come back through tomorrow."

"Aight, bet! This shit is easy money, Lyric. Easy as shit."

"That's what I heard."

I glanced around the room at the unfamiliar faces. Some barely paid any attention to me while others gave me too much of it. I kept my eyes on the ones I needed to as Quandra walked me back out to my car. The street lights had just come on, and the apartment complex suddenly was littered with men and women outside, listening to loud music with little kids running around shirtless in saggy diapers. "I'll see you tomorrow, Lyric," Quandra said as I got into my car and headed out. I was warned about trusting Quandra last time, but I went against it, and she burned me in the end. Even though it seemed like everything was squashed between us and a new beginning just started, I still kept one eye on her. Everything seemed cool, but the pursuit of money is the root of all evil and every woman in that apartment wanted their cut, including me.

Chapter 2

      I got home at 1 am. I went to the store for about an hour while I waited to come down off my high. I didn't want to bring that around Prince or Mrs. Butler, so I had to make sure I was in my right state of mind when I saw them. I dropped a little bit of Visine into my eyes and waited in the parking lot of my apartment complex for a few minutes until the redness of my eyes were completely white. I bought a shirt from Walmart when I was there and got rid of the one that was soaked in the scent of marijuana. Even though she wasn't my biological mother, I still felt like she would scold me for coming home smelling like weed. I had that much respect for her, even in my own house.

      Prince was asleep when I walked through the door, but Mrs. Butler was wide awake, flipping through channels on the television I bought earlier that week. "Honey, you have to hurry up and get cable or something in this house. There is literally nothing on here to watch," she said as she pressed the buttons on the remote. I walked over to her and flipped to a station that played all the old-school television shows. *Good Times, Facts of Life, What's Happening,* and *What's Happening Now,* just to name a few. Her eyes lit up, "I didn't know you had this channel," she said as the *Good Times* theme song came on. I plopped down next to her.

"Yeah, you can't reach it if you just flip through the channels. For some reason, the antenna won't pick it up unless you actually punch in the station with the remote."

"Duly noted," she said as J.J. came onto the screen, telling everybody he was the prince of the ghetto.

"How was Prince today?"

"Prince? Oh, that boy was all right. He is teething so he was a little fussier than normal, but Grandma knows how to handle that, so he was alright. What about you? You were gone for quite some time."

"Oh, yeah. I was just, um, out looking for work."

"Work?" she asked quizzically, "I thought you had enough money saved up for a year?"

"Oh, I do. I just hate sitting around the house. I forgot how much I hated that in the process of leaving Milwaukee. I've only been down here for a little while, and I'm already getting antsy."

"Well, what will you do with Prince if you start working?"

"Well, Mom. I thought that maybe you could stay out here for a little while. I mean, if you weren't doing anything else."

She looked at me with a side-eye, "How long, Lyric?"

"I don't know, maybe a month or two. Just until I can find Prince a trustworthy daycare or something like that."

J.J.'s dad threatened him while Michael laughed in the background. The audience's laughter followed soon after his. I felt her eyes on me as I peered at the television. I was always able to feel someone looking at me and honestly, it was a little creepy at times, but I guess it was a sixth sense for me. I always figured it was just my mama or Big Mama warning me about someone, and now, it was happening more than it ever did before.

"Lyric, you aren't out here getting into any mess again, are you?"

"No, Ma'am."

She paused, attempting to feel me out. I kept my eyes away from her, "Alright," she said, "because that is the last thing you need to do. Out of the frying pan and into the fire, you know? But I'm going to trust you and your judgment out here. Oh," she continued, "and to answer your question, I will stay out here for as long as you need me to watch Prince. Depending on your work schedule, I may have to take him back to Milwaukee with me from time to time just to check on things, but I will let you know ahead of time. You just let me know about a week before you are supposed to start so I can make plans, alright?"

"Yes, ma'am."

"Alright."

I leaned back on my couch as she laughed at the sitcom on the television. As I closed my eyes, I couldn't help but think about how I was becoming prone to always finding myself in the most troubling situations. From Junie to Nas and even until now, I was always around violence. Maybe I was just more susceptible to it than anyone else, or perhaps, I was just too selfish to see that my involvement in these types of things not only affected me but those around me as well.

I heard voices coming from the kitchen when I woke up. Stacey and Prince were nowhere around me when I tossed the covers onto the floor and headed into the bright-lit kitchen.

"No, honey, that is way too much salt! You'll mess around and send all of our blood pressures through the roof! Mama is not eating that; you will have to make another pot."

Big Mama walked over to the cabinet and grabbed another large pot from the shelf. She spoke to me without even glancing in my direction, "Lyric, baby; I hope you don't plan on standing there the whole time and leaving your mother and me to do all the work. Get yo' lazy behind over here and help us!" I rubbed my eyes, thinking everything would disappear as soon as I refocused, but both of them were still there. "Hey, sweetie," my mother said as she dumped the pot of ground beef out into the trash, "I never was as good of a cook as Mama is. She's trying to teach me some stuff that I should have taken the time to learn when I was younger." She rinsed the pot out and placed it back on the stove as I looked around to see what they needed me to do. Big Mama stood in front of me with her hands on her hips, her gray eyes seemed to glow. "Lyric? Baby, what's wrong? You look like you've seen a ghost." With that, she walked back over to Mama and showed her how to season the food without ruining it.

I walked over and stood just behind them, still trying to piece together what was going on. It was surreal and even though I knew it was a dream I struggled to believe it. "Ok, now," Mama said, "I got it." She sprinkled a little bit of salt in her hand and spread it evenly over the meat she just placed inside the pot. "What are y'all making?" I asked nervously.

"I'm teaching your lazy old mother how to make lasagna without giving everybody in the house high blood pressure. You know, one thing she is doing now is actually listening to my advice. When she was younger, she didn't do any of that but now that she is older, she seems like she can't get enough of it."

"Well, Mama, you know I was hard-headed. I had to learn things my way, and it was usually the hard way."

"Umm-hmm," she peered at me, "that is where this one gets it from. Lyric, sit your behind down at the table."

"Big Mama, I thought you—"

"Girl, sit!"

I looked at my mother, "Girl, I don't know why you're staring at me. You better sit down at that table before Big Mama tans your behind." I was still intimidated by Big Mama, even beyond the grave. I sat down in my seat, and she pulled out a chair and sat right across from me. She gazed into my eyes for a few moments, not saying a word. I beheld the fullness of her eyes, and suddenly snapshots of future events flashed within her irises like cut scenes in movies. They were pictures of me lying in hospital beds, shooting pistols, and doing questionable things with men and women. Just then, they returned back to their original color, and my mom came and sat by her side. She no longer looked like the surprised woman on the photo on Big Mama's dresser; she was a spitting image of her mother.

"So, you don't think we know what's going on, do you? We don't see all things, but the good Lord allowed us to keep a watch on what you are doing, and he even let us come down here to talk to you."

I didn't know how to respond to her. For the moment, it was all too weird for me to make sense of it.

"Don't sit there with your face all scrunched up; you know why we are here. That Quandra who you ran into the other day? You know she is no good!"

Mama chimed in, "I knew it myself. I had a friend like her in my younger days, and she got me into a lot of trouble when I wasn't trying to. Lyric, you have to resist that urge to want to get involved in trouble. I know you get bored easily because you're just like me, but you have to find something else to do. Prince is there. You're in a new city, and it is a fresh new start. You don't need to be going down the same path you did in Milwaukee."

"Tell her, baby! Tell this hard-headed old grandchild of mine! She seems like she doesn't have a lick of sense anymore!"

"I'm telling her, Mama! But I can't make the girl do what I say; she is going to do what she wants either way. I know it because it's my daughter and I did the same thing to you. Maybe it's karma."

"Oh, hush up! I don't believe in that old voodoo mess!" She looked at me, "Now listen here, Lyric. If you keep going the way you're going, then you will be headed for some things that you will never recover from. Big Mama has seen it all when I was down here, baby, I've seen it all. The Lord is patient, though; he is indeed patient, but that doesn't mean he will strive with you forever. You need to get back to doing something positive with your life. The way you were going before you met that old knucklehead. What's.... what's that boy name again? Nas, that's right, before you met Nas."

The meat on the stove began smoking, "Oh dear Lord, child, you are going to burn Lyric's place down!" My mama rushed to the stove,

"Mama! I was sitting here talking with y'all now, don't start fussing at me!"

"Well, you need to know how to multi-task!" Big Mama insisted.

As they went back and forth, I imagined that this is how life would have been if they were both still alive. The love and bickering while cooking hot meals and trying to keep me on the right path. I smiled at the bittersweet thought, knowing that it would be over as soon as I opened my eyes. Big Mama never liked Quandra and on the day I went to Chicago with her she warned me about it, but I ignored her and did what I wanted. That's usually how things went—I received advice but still had to learn the hard way. "Now Lyric, don't think I am finished with you," Big Mama said as she stirred meat inside the pot, "and I know you're hard-headed behind is going to do what you want anyway but this is a warning, hear?"

She put the spoon down and turned towards me as darkness in the room blacked everything out but her, "The devil is after you just like the good Lord is, and he wants you just as bad. You've got to make a choice one way or the other, hear? You can go back into that life if you want to but just know that it won't turn out good. No sir, not this time."

Just then, I felt a tugging on my shirt. When I opened my eyes, Prince stood in front of me with a slobbery smile as Stacey watched from her seat. "He kept calling for his mama, so I let him go on over there and wake you up." I smiled and picked him up onto the couch with me while his cooing filled the room. My future sat right next to me, and I knew he was all I needed, but for some reason I wanted more. I couldn't handle just sitting around or even working a regular 40-hour a week job for the rest of my life. As much as people would kill for a new start, I had it, and I knew I couldn't just throw it away without at least trying to live a decent life first. Prince leaned in and placed a wet, slobbery kiss on my cheek, and I smiled as Big Mama's warning echoed in my mind. I had to try it at least because like everybody told me, this was not about me anymore. This was about Prince and his future as well.

Chapter 3

I called Quandra early the next day and let her know I wasn't going to make it over there. "Oh, well aight, girl. I know Malley is gonna be a little salty and shit but if you ever decide to come through, just let a bitch know. We'll be lookin' for you." I could hear the disappointment in her voice, but I had to at least try the legit way out first while I was here. I owed it to myself but more importantly, I owed it to Prince and Big Mama.

I ended up getting a job as a cashier at the grocery store not too far from my apartment. It was one of the few places who would actually hire me with little to no experience, but I picked up on shit fast. There were mostly high schoolers who worked there with a few adults who looked as if they made some fucked up choices earlier in their lives that caused them to work full time here. Shit, I was in the same boat so there wasn't much I could say about that myself. The hardest part about the job was forcing fake ass smiles whenever people came through my line. I wasn't used to that shit, but more importantly, I wasn't used to people telling me what to do, and that is exactly what one of the supervisors seemed to get a kick out of doing.

Charlene Tate was the woman that was directly above me and she was known to power trip. She watched me like a hawk and waited with a pen and notepad in her hand to write me up for whatever bullshit she could.

"Uh, Lyric, what are you doing?"

"I'm working."

"No, you're not working. You were on your phone; I see it right there on the counter."

"We can have our phones out."

"Not when there are things to do."

She stood to the side of me, the bottom of her pants just above her ankles and her gut sticking out just as much as her stomach did. Her fat cheeks were plump, causing her eyes to look buttoned to her face. Acne littered the sides of her face like trash in the alleys of inner city neighborhoods, and she behaved as if she took the anger from everything that went wrong in her life out on those who were under her.

"Charlene, there hasn't been anybody in my line in the past fifteen minutes and my aisle is clean. What else is there for me to do?"

She checked my line, and after she realized everything was in order, she pointed to the aisle behind me, "Well, what about that one?"

"What one?"

"The aisle behind you."

"That is not my responsibility."

"It is now. Clean it up."

With that, she spun around and walked away leaving me to do a job that wasn't even my duty and it added to the growing list of reasons that I didn't like her and felt my knees buckling under the monotony of the job. Every time I wanted to just pack up and walk out, I thought about Prince, and for the time being the images that flooded through my mind were sharp enough to keep me in my place. Things weren't going as smoothly as I wanted them to go, but by the third week I had become accustomed to most things that happened there. I unintentionally became friends with a few people there.

Cedrick was a younger guy who just graduated from high school. He just turned eighteen, and he was attractive, baby face and all. His light brown eyes always found a way to make me smile, even on my hardest days, and he tried to run his little game on me a few times, but after he realized that shit wasn't moving with me, he backed up. He reminded me a lot of Vinny, the way he tried to be hard but in reality, he was just a regular guy that allowed the music he heard to shape his thought process. Alisha was a 16-year-old who was just as sick of Charlene as I was. She had a feisty attitude, but she was so much of a girly girl that it annoyed me at times. She had the mentality of a stuck up, light-skinned female but her appearance didn't match what she thought of herself. She was thick as fuck though so most niggas pumped her head up and because of that, nobody could tell her shit.

We were all chilling in the break room as they were telling me the shit that was going on with the kids on their blocks. Cedrick did his best to paint pictures of a gutter ass hood life just to try to impress me, but I saw right through his stories. The shit that he came up with was so outlandish that, even if I didn't know about the gutter side of life, I still might not have believed him.

"So, yeah, Lyric, I was sittin' there and shit and then out of nowhere, like five niggas rolled up and me and my guys. So, I stood up, and I was like, 'what the fuck?' you know what I'm sayin'? Because I wasn't gonna let no niggas just roll up on us like that and then out of nowhere, this nigga pulled out and let off like nine shots and shit."

Alisha interrupted him, "Nine shots? For real?"

"Hell yeah! The nigga was aiming at the homie that was behind me and shit, but he missed. I pushed his gun down, and then I pulled out and bussed, and the nigga started running."

"Daaaaaamn."

I interrupted him, "What kind of gun was it?"

"Shit, I don't know," he said, "it was just a regular Glock I guess."

"He could fit it in one hand?"

"Yeah."

I laughed, "You lying ass little boy. A fucking Glock only holds seven bullets with one in the chamber."

There was a brief pause. "Shit, I said I think it was a Glock! I'm not sure, though!"

"Bullshit, you little ass nigga," I said laughing.

Alisha joined in, "I knew that shit was sounding too fucking impossible. Nine fucking shots right by your ear and you didn't go deaf, nigga? Those gunshots are loud as hell."

He looked between both of us and said, "Man, fuck y'all! My life was in danger, and y'all are looking for inconsistencies in my story and shit! Fuck y'all!"

Alisha and I laughed out loud as Charlene walked in with a pen and notepad in her hand, "Umm, I think your breaks are over," she said, glaring at her watch. Alisha spoke up, "Ugh, you always coming in here trying to regulate shit. Break ain't even over yet; I know I got one minute left." Charlene sucked her teeth, "Um, no. You left at 11:14 am, and it is now 11:25 am. You need to get back out there." Alisha huffed and walked out of the break room as Cedrick followed right behind her. She turned her attention towards me, "Shouldn't you be clocking in now?" I leaned back in my chair and plopped my feet onto the table.

"No, I don't start until 11:30 and you know it, so why don't you go and do your job instead of sweating me for no ass reason."

"You heard me."

"I'm going to write you up."

"Bullshit, you can't write me up when I'm not even on my shift yet. I got four minutes before I even need to be out there; so like I said, you need to go ahead and do your job instead of sweating me off the clock."

She scowled in my direction, wanting to say something else but knowing she wasn't in a position to do so. With that, she turned around and stormed out of the break room, bumping into chairs and tables accidentally because of her wideness. I knew she was going to have her attention on me even more but shit, it wouldn't be any different from any other day. I peeked at my phone one last time before I went to clock in. Prince was my screen saver as he sat there looking more and more like Nas and less like Junie every day. From what Vinny told me, Nas was close to getting out of prison, but I had a good feeling that he didn't know where I was. I still didn't know what was up with Loc that day he was supposed to take me out of town, and I didn't care. If he was going to set me up, he was going to have to try another way because I made sure I stayed one step ahead of him and whoever else was trying to get to me.

Later that day, Quandra and Malley popped up at my job. They strolled into my line with a few items and slid them onto the conveyor belt. "Whassup, Lyric?" Quandra said as she stood in front of me. I shook my head, slightly embarrassed that they saw me this way. "Shit. Just up here working." Malley smiled, her fire red hair was pulled into a ponytail, and her makeup was flawlessly painted onto her face. She looked as if she was on her way to a photoshoot.

"Working?" she said as she shook her head, "damn. I mean, you can't be enjoying yourself up here."

"Shit, it's paying the bills, so I can't complain too much."

"Well, you're better than me," Quandra chimed in, "I ain't built for this type of shit. Standing all day and listening to these bitching ass customers complain about prices all fucking day. I don't know how you do it, Lyric."

"I don't either," Malley said, "especially when you have the opportunity to make more than, what, $9 an hour or whatever dimes and nickels they are throwing at you up here."

They laughed as I scanned their items, trying to block them out. Images of Prince flooded my mind as I refocused on the reason I was still there. The reason I kept putting up with Charlene's disrespectful, power tripping ass. I knew the opportunity to make more money was out there, but I convinced myself that this is the route that I needed to take.

"$27.49, y'all."

"Quandra, you got that?"

"Damn, bitch. It's thirty fucking dollars; you ain't got it?"

"Quandra, I got the shit last time. Yo' ass the one high as fuck with the munchies."

"Fuuuuuck," Quandra said, sliding the money into my hand.

Moments later, Charlene walked into my aisle. "Um, excuse me, Lyric? Your line is filling with people and now is not the time to be carrying unnecessary conversations with your little friends. Smile, ring them up, and get to the next person in line." Malley scrunched her eyebrows up, "Damn, we been in this lane for like two minutes and shit. Chill the fuck out." Charlene put her hands on her hips, "Excuse me, ma'am; this doesn't concern you, alright?" Malley raised her eyebrows and looked at me, waiting to hear what I said next. "Charlene, I'm moving through the line, aight? The fact that you're standing here interrupting me is the only thing that is making me take longer." She took out her notepad, "Oh really?" she said, writing something down, "is there anything else you want to say?"

I glanced over at Quandra and Malley as they stood there, glaring incredulously at Charlene. Suddenly, thoughts began to take over every image of Prince that I tried to force myself to see. I was immediately torn between two choices, and it was at that moment that I felt that I tried. I gave it three weeks, and as Malley and Quandra stood in front of me not answering to anyone but themselves, I envied that even more. I wanted that life, and if it could come without the crime, then I would have taken it, but right now, it didn't, and I didn't have time to wait for it. Charlene tapped her foot onto the floor with the pen and paper in her hand, "Well, Lyric? Do YOU have anything else to say? I know you hear me talking to you? Are you done trying to show off in front of your little friends or what?"

Before I knew it, every positive image in my mind blacked out, and it was replaced with the venom I had been holding onto for weeks. I was already on the fence about whether to stay or leave but seeing Quandra and Malley in line was enough to push me over and suddenly words that I'd been holding onto for weeks flowed out,

"Bitch, let me tell yo' fat ass something. I don't know who the fuck bullied yo' ass in high school, but I'm telling you right now that I'm done lettin' you talk to me any kind of way. Yo' hungry hungry hippo lookin' ass need to back the fuck away from me before I kick you in the fucking stomach and make those doughnuts fall out your pocket, bitch. I held my tongue for this long and you lucky I didn't beat the fuck out of you by now with yo' fat ass. Fuck you and fuck this job, bitch."

With that, I snatched my nametag off and threw it onto the register. "Now, you ring the rest of these muthafuckas up, and you better do it in less than two minutes, you fat ass bitch." I heard Quandra and Malley laughing out loud as everyone in the store fixed their attention on me in complete silence. At least I could say I tried and didn't just jump head first into the life that I left behind in Milwaukee. I felt Big Mama's tears falling into my heart as I calmly walked out of the store. "Lyric!" Quandra yelled out, "Bitch, you never gave us our change! Bring yo' ass back here with our money!" she said as her laughter followed me out of the store. *Fuck that*, I said to myself; I was just going to have to give it back to her when I saw her later and at this rate, that was definitely going to happen.

I walked into the house as Stacey held Prince in her lap. He cooed when I went into the front room, and she looked at her watch, "Lyric, baby? You're home early. Everything ok."

I sighed and plopped down onto the couch, "I couldn't do it, Mama. I just couldn't stay there and work that job while somebody was always in my ear telling me what to do." She looked concerned.

"What happened?"

"I quit."

"Lyric," she said as Prince crawled to me, "it was only three weeks."

I picked him up off the floor, "I know, Mama. I know, I just couldn't deal with it. I don't know how people go to work and deal with people like that. I just couldn't do it."

"Charlene was still mistreating you?"

"Yeah, but not just me. Just a few people that were under her supervision."

"Lyric, did you just walk out or what?"

"No, Mama. I cussed her out."

"Lyric! You did not!"

"Yes, I did. I told her fat self to get away from me before I kicked her in the stomach and made the doughnuts fall out her pocket."

She covered her mouth, "No you didn't, Lyric." Prince slapped one of his toys against my chest, "I did, Mama." Moments later, she burst out laughing and in turn, she made me laugh right along with her. "It's not funny, Mama. She was so annoying." She caught her breath, "I'm sorry, Lyric. You're right; it's not funny, but then again, it is!" I was upset all the way home but seeing Prince and hearing her laugh helped to lighten the situation. After a few more moments, she collected herself enough to ask,

"Ok, well, what are you going to do now?"

"I don't know yet. I mean, I think I have another job lined up, but I'm thinking about whether I should take it or not."

"Where?"

I hesitated, "Um, it's another store. A clothing store, though."

"Maybe you shouldn't work in retail, baby. You should apply for some entry level positions at a call center or something. They usually do pretty good at hiring people with no experience as long as you have a high school diploma."

The words she said went in one ear and out the other because, no matter what, I couldn't see myself going to another position where I had to take orders from someone else. I wasn't good in a subordinate position and, in my heart, I knew it. I leaned over and kissed Prince on his cheek as he smiled, causing me to think about Nas and long for the times that we were in love with each other. The moments he treated me like his queen when we ran the city together were some of the best moments of my life. I sighed as Prince slobbered onto my shirt.

"Well, Lyric, whatever you decide, I'm proud of you. The way you've moved away and turned over a new leaf is admirable, and I know you have made Big Mama proud. I'm going to go in here and cook something for dinner," she said as she got up to head towards the kitchen, "Oh, and Serena may come by later this week. Her cousins have been staying with her at the house, but she says she misses us and wants to see Prince."

"Ok, that's fine."

As she walked into the kitchen, I took a deep breath and slowly exhaled. Moments later, Quandra sent me a text, *Whenever U R ready, we will be here waiting. If U want to come through this weekend, just let me know. Aight?* I sat, looking at the text message while Prince did everything in his power to grab my phone out of my hand. If Big Mama was here physically then maybe her presence would have been enough to deter me, but right now, I felt as if I was going down a slippery slope and couldn't do anything to stop myself even though I wanted to. It was like I was watching myself make dumb decisions, and there was nothing I could do about it. After a while, I responded to her, *Aight.*

I closed my phone and tossed it onto the couch as Prince began whining and wouldn't stop until he got my phone in his hands. I sat him on the floor and walked over to the window that overlooked the parking lot of my apartment complex. I smirked at my reflection in the mirror when I realized that I looked exactly like my mother in the picture on Big Mama's dresser. I mirrored her expression; the wide-eyed look that made it seem like she was caught by surprise. The only thing I needed in my hand was a cigarette, and there wouldn't be anyone who could tell us apart. "Well, Big Mama, I guess I should apologize now," I said, looking up to the sky, "you already warned me, but I really don't know what else to do. You already know that I can't work a regular job, and at least I tried. I tried, Big Mama, I really did, but I just couldn't do it. Maybe I'm just prone to live this kind of life, you know? Maybe this is just the way things are supposed to go. I don't know, but right now, all I can tell you is that I'm sorry for disappointing you or whatever else I've done. I love you, ok? I really do, and I just hope that you can forgive me."

I wiped a tear from my eye as Stacey came back in the room, "Lyric, honey? Are you alright?" I kept my eyes focused in front of me, "Oh, yeah Mama, I'm alright. I was just talking to myself." There were a few moments of silence before she spoke again, "Okay. Prince has your phone, and he was on his way to dump it into the toilet before I caught him." I laughed, "That little boy! Thanks for grabbing him." Suddenly, I felt her hand around my waist. The touch caused me to jump and turn around as she stood right next to me. I couldn't hide my teary eyes from her.

"Are you sure you're alright?" she asked, solemnly.

I sighed, "I just miss Big Mama, you know? It seems like I won't be able to live up to what she wanted me to be."

"Oh, Lyric, honey," she said, wrapping her arms around me, "Trust me. Like I said, Big Mama is proud of you. I know she is, and I know she misses you just as much. You just keep doing what you're doing, and I promise you everything will be okay."

The tighter she squeezed, the more I felt like a failure. Prince looked over at me as he stood at the table, the usual smile that was plastered on his face was nonexistent this time around and for an instant, it felt as if he knew what I was about to get into. It seemed that he felt the selfishness that was beating inside my heart and there was nothing I could do about it. I turned my head away from him and leaned it on Stacey's shoulder. *At least I tried*, I said to myself, *at least I tried*.

Chapter 4

The sun shined brightly through the blinds when I woke up the next morning. A thick silence coated the house as I laid on my back adjusting my eyes to the glare shooting into the living room. When I sat up, I called out for Stacey, but my voice echoed off the walls, and there was no response. Lazily, I walked throughout the house searching for any sign of Prince or Stacey, but to my surprise they were nowhere to be seen. "Prince?" I called out his name as if he was old enough to respond back to me. The kitchen was spotless, and both the bed in my room and Prince's room were made up perfectly. The covers were tucked sternly across the mattresses, and all of Prince's toys were placed in his bin. I just figured that Stacey took him somewhere earlier that morning, so I didn't think anything of it. She was known just to get up and go with him sometimes, especially since I had begun working. They would both be up and out of the house or preparing to leave before I left to go to work.

I went back down into the living room, plopped onto the couch, and flipped on the television. There was breaking news on every station, all of them covering the same story.

"There was a shootout on the north side of Milwaukee today involving at least a dozen police officers and over a dozen black men who are believed to be members of a street gang. The casualties have not been confirmed, but there are thought to be at least seven at the minimal."

The camera man zoomed in on the area where the shootout took place, and when everything was in focus, I couldn't believe what I saw. "That's Big Mama's house," I said in horror as I scooted forward on the couch. Yellow tape circled around the trees in front of the house, and my hands shook uncontrollably as I reached for my phone. Vinny didn't answer and with that, my heart just about leaped out of my chest through my mouth. I pulled myself to my feet as the room spun, causing me to stumble as I made my way to the front door. When I opened it, Nas was outside leaning against my car. He smiled, "Oh, shit! Look who finally decided to come out the crib. Lyric, aka, Suzy Muthafuckin' Rock." I held onto the banister to regain my balance, completely in disbelief at what I was seeing. Loc and Man-Man stood to the left and the right of him as he stood up. "Shit," he continued, "I thought you were at Big Mama's house. I would've never sent the fellas to the crib had I known you were here." I looked at the parking lot, but there was nobody else in sight.

"Come on down here. I mean, we obviously got shit we need to discuss."

"How the hell did you find me?"

He laughed, "Well, yo boy Vinny? He told us. I mean, the information didn't come out quickly at all. That nigga really had a love for you; you know what I'm saying? He held off for as long as he could, but you know how I am, right?"

"The fuck did you do to him?"

"Don't worry about that nigga. He is no longer in pain, you know what I'm saying? I wasn't gonna let the nigga suffer any more than he had to. I mean, I'm not completely heartless."

Tears rushed to my eyes as I reached for the pistol on my hip that was no longer there. Nas walked closer to the staircase with a cruel smile on his face as I backed into the door but somehow it had locked when it shut behind me. Suddenly, a young boy appeared to my left and began walking towards Nas. I squinted my eyes, trying to make his face clearer as he walked closer to us with his hand inside his pocket. *Cedrick*, I thought to myself as he kept coming. Loc and Man-Man gripped their pistols as Nas turned in his direction. "Who the fuck is this little nigga?" Nas asked rhetorically. When he was close enough to us, his face became more distinguishable. His lips, the shape of his eyes, and his walk all pointed to one person. "Junie?" I yelled out loud and just then, the young man smiled. His dimple pushed one of his cheeks in as Nas looked perplexed at what he was seeing.

That's when Nas smiled and walked over to him. The two of them embraced each other, and I didn't understand what was happening. *That can't be Junie*, I said to myself and even though I believed it was him, I knew it wasn't. They looked just alike though and for a moment, my mind couldn't tell the two apart. Nas turned around towards me with his arm around the young man and just then, he finally looked directly at me. I squinted my eyes, "Prince?" I said in disbelief as he stood next to his father. "Who the fuck did you think it was?" Nas said, "Junie? Junie is fucking dead and you know it. But this right here? This is my son. Not Junie's, aight? But I understand how you feel about that nigga. I know that you still love him and shit, and you probably put him in my place sometimes while you were with me. As a matter of fact," he pulled out a pistol and aimed it at me, "I know that there is one person that you would do anything for. One person that you would end your whole life just to protect."

Suddenly, the sun's rays began fading out of the sky and dark clouds covered the horizon. The birds that were once chirping had gone completely silent and both Loc and Man-Man were gone. It was just the three of us standing outside. "Now look, one big happy family, Lyric. This is what you wanted, right?" he chambered a bullet, "I mean, if you had your choice, it would probably be Junie standing in my spot, but hey, you got his brother, so I guess that's close enough, huh? You know where you fucked up, though? You let me know your weakness. You let me know the one way I could get to you—and me? I don't want weaknesses anymore. You were my weakness for a second. Prince was my weakness, and well, I know you are going to hate this, but I had to get rid of both of you. I got Prince kidnapped but yo' ass," he laughed, "yo' ass ruined all that shit by going to find him. Not only that, you fucking left town with him, too. It took me a little longer to find you, though, but there is nothing I can't find. So, now we're here. And I could just kill you right now." He laughed, "Well, I should just kill you now, but you know how I am. I like to see bitches suffer before I send them out this muthafucka, you know? Like poison. A slow death, bitch. I'ma make sure you die a slow fuckin' death."

He stood with the pistol aimed at me as I held onto the banister, still woozy, trying to make my way down the stairs but stumbling with each step. The volume of his laughter increased as I took each step, struggling to keep my balance. Suddenly, a gunshot went off, and I ducked my head. When I lifted it, Prince stopped smiling. He dropped to his knees and fell over onto the concrete as blood gushed from his head. Nas's laughter became louder as I screamed Prince's name loud enough to wake the dead. Nas fired three more shots into his body, and I fell down the rest of the stairs as my legs turned to jelly. He walked out, laughing, as I crawled over to Prince and he laid there with his eyes wide open, blood flowing from his mouth and the hole in the side of his head. I threw my arms around him and yelled out his name louder, begging for someone to come help, but nobody came. There wasn't an ambulance horn or police siren to be heard as I laid there with my head on my son's chest. "Kill me!" I yelled out to Nas as he walked away laughing. "Just kill me! Kill me right now!"

I leaped up from the couch as Prince stood in front of me with a toy truck in his hand. If I had stayed asleep any longer, I'm sure he would have clocked me with it. I immediately reached out to him and wrapped him in my arms as he giggled and tears flowed from my eyes. I rocked him back and forth in my arms, clenching onto him as if it was the last time I was going to see him. "Oh, he's in here," Stacey said as she stood just outside the room, "I'm going to head to sleep. Let me know if you need anything, alright Lyric?" I shook my head to let her know that I heard her so she wouldn't come to me and try to get me to talk.

I lost track of time, and before I knew it, Prince was asleep with his head resting on my shoulder. The tears hadn't stopped coming from my eyes since I woke up and all I could think about was Nas. The dreams I had were usually given to me for a reason and this time I couldn't help but wonder: Was Nas trying to get us out of town so he could kill both of us? Was Prince's kidnapping something that he set up on his own to trap me? I remembered how he told me that having a family was a weakness, and with more people coming into Milwaukee to threaten his throne, I knew that we had to be on our way to becoming a liability to him. I could tell by the way he spoke to me, and maybe that is what caused him to change towards me. If I had to put money on that being the reason, I would put everything I owned.

If the dream was real, then I knew what I had to do at this point. Now, it wasn't about me—it was about Prince. I didn't want to believe that Nas was ruthless enough to hurt Prince, and I didn't think he was, but I wouldn't put anything past him. He always told me that he wanted a son to carry his name. He wanted somebody that he could pass his legacy to whenever he died, so I didn't think it was possible for him just to switch like that but if he did it to me, then I knew he could turn on anybody else. I laid Prince down next to me and shut off everything in the front room, then repositioned myself back on the couch. I had to figure something out and I had to do it quickly because if everything in the dream was real, I had to be a step ahead of Nas and stop the shit before it had a chance to start.

Chapter 5

The next morning, I woke up after Prince repeatedly backhanded me in my face as he slept. He was a wild sleeper and even though the couch was a decent size, he still found a way to get his hands on my cheeks. I rolled off the sofa and tucked him back in as I walked into the kitchen. Stacey sat at the table with a somber look on her face. "Mom," I asked, "are you alright?" She looked towards me as if I startled her with my voice and said, "Oh, no, I'm fine baby, I am completely okay." She stood up from the table and walked to the refrigerator before continuing,

"I see you put up with Prince and his wild sleeping habits last night."

"Oh. Yeah, I just didn't feel like taking him back to his bed. I forgot how crazy he could get."

"Girl, who are you telling? I wake up with arms, legs, hands and feet in my face whenever I decide to let that little boy sleep with me."

"Yeah, he is a wild one."

"It just cracks me up because Junie slept the same way. The exact same way."

She pulled a jug of milk out and grabbed a box of cereal while I sat down at the table.

"You want a bowl?" she asked.

"Yeah, I'll take one."

We took turns pouring milk and cereal, remaining silent the whole time. It was odd because she usually had a lot to say but I could tell something was weighing her down. I was never one to force people to talk because I hated when it was done to me, so I glared at the back of the cereal box, giving her the chance to speak up when she was ready. She never did, and moments later, my phone rang. I walked into the front room and picked it up.

"Whassup Vinny?"

"Yo, you're at apartment 536, right?"

"Yeah, why?"

Moments later, there were knocks at the door. I opened it up, and Vinny stood on the other side. "What the fuck is up, nigga!?" he yelled out as I threw my arms around him. "Man, what's good, Vinny! Shit! It feels like I haven't seen you in forever!" I released him as he walked inside, "I know. Shit is boring as hell around the crib without y'all there." He walked over to Prince and bothered him until he woke up. Once he realized Vinny sat in front of him, he sat up and reached for him as Vinny embraced him back, "Damn, little nigga! I missed you the most! Don't tell yo mama, though, you know how she gets." I sat down across from him, smiling at their interaction,

"Shut up, nigga! But man, what's been up!? You just makin' surprise visits on niggas now, huh?"

"Yeah, you know? I just wanted to sneak up on y'all and shit, you know? See how you like yo' new life."

"Man, this shit is for the birds, fam, for real. I had a regular ass job, and shit and I quit like three weeks later."

"I remember you telling me about that. It was at the grocery story, right?"

"Hell yeah. That shit was a mistake from day fuckin' one, bro."

"I already knew it wasn't gonna work out for you. I bet you cussed somebody out, didn't you?"

I laughed, "You know me."

Just then, Stacey walked into the living room. Vinny looked at her as she came in and his eyes widened. I knew what kind of look that was because Stacey was a very attractive older woman and she only looked to be half her age. To this point, Vinny had only heard about her but he had never seen her. "And who is this young lady?" he asked me while he peered at her. "That is Prince's grandmother." He turned towards me, "Grandmother?" Stacey walked over to Vinny and extended her hand, "Oh, hush, Lyric! That makes me sound so much older," she shook Vinny's hand, "I am Prince's G-Ma." Vinny smiled, "Well, G-Ma, I'm Prince's uncle/Godfather. I heard so much about you, and it is a pleasure to see you finally, uh, I mean meet you."

Stacey smiled at his flirtatiousness then glanced at me,

"Lyric, baby, I'm a little tired. Whenever you get finished with Vinny here, can you come to the room? I need to talk to you."

"You want me to come now?"

"No, no baby. You go ahead and finish up here. I can wait."

"Alright."

Vinny had his eyes glued on her ass while she walked away. I shook my head, "Damn nigga, stop undressing her with your eyes." He laughed, "Man, I didn't know she was that fine! Shit!" Prince started whining, and moments later, Stacey came back in with his bottle and took him out the room with her. Vinny didn't speak again until she left, "So, you know Nas is out, right?" A look of concern flooded my face, "He out? What do you mean? How he get out?"

"Shit, his lawyer got his case dropped somehow. I don't know the details all I know is that nigga is out."

"For how long?"

"I don't know," he looked around the room, "but it's been some weird shit happening at the crib. Like, doors being left unlocked that I know I locked, and it just feels like somebody else be in the fucking crib sometimes."

"What? You ain't talking about no ghosts and shit, are you Vinny? Cuz you know how you can get."

"Nah, Lyric, this ain't no fucking ghost... and fuck you but seriously, though, shit is weird. Alarms ain't going off or nothing though so I just figured I was trippin', you know what I'm saying?"

"You stay there by yourself?"

"Yeah. Well, I mean, I have some people there from time to time, but I know them, you know what I'm saying? I know they're not on no bullshit."

"Well, maybe it's them."

"Yeah, I thought so myself. It could be them, but I just wanted to let you know that Nas was out and shit."

"You came all way here to tell me that?"

"Hell naw, I came here to see y'all! Got-damn, Lyric! A nigga drives a couple hours to come kick it with you, and you make me regret it and shit."

"Awwww, quit bein sensitive, nigga!"

We sat and talked with each other for a few hours before we went to grab a bite to eat. It was good seeing him, and I don't know what it was but from time to time, I imagined what it would be like if we weren't like brother and sister. The thoughts of him sliding between my legs crept in and out of my mind throughout the time he was with me, and I let my mind run wild with it before I tried to block it out. Maybe it was the fact that I hadn't had sex since Nas fucked me in jail a long ass time ago. As a matter of fact, I knew that is what it was, but even then, I couldn't stop my imagination from wandering. When it came time for him to leave, I hugged him a little tighter than usual. He looked at me oddly, "Uh, Lyric? You aight?" I quickly released him and cleared my throat, "Um, yeah. Yeah,

I'm good. I just missed you, I guess." He laughed with a hint of uncertainty, "Oh, aight. Well, I umm... missed you, too?" He said it as if he was unsure whether he should say it or not and I understood why. For as long as he knew me, I wasn't the type to talk that way to him, and I knew it came off weird to him.

"Whatever, nigga. Yo, just let me know when you get to the crib, aight?"

"No doubt."

With that, he was gone. He only spent about half the day with us, but that was long enough for me. I could only hope and pray that he was going to be alright back in Milwaukee and even though we both came up with logical explanations for the so-called weird shit that was happening back at the house, there was still those *What if* thoughts that flooded through my mind. When his car disappeared out of the parking lot, I headed back to the apartment and made my way up to my room to talk to Stacey. I figured that she finally wanted to talk about whatever was bothering her earlier that morning.

When I got into the room, Stacey sat on the bed staring off into nothing as Prince laid asleep right next to her. She was startled when I walked in just like she was earlier, "Oh, Lyric. My goodness, I didn't even hear you come in." I sat down on the bed right next to her and moments later, she reached towards my hand and held onto it firmly.

"What's up, Mom?"

She sighed, "I have something to tell you, and I know you're going to be upset, but it will explain a lot."

I repositioned myself in the bed and waited for her to speak. "Well, you know back when I was telling you that I had a friend down at the police station, and she asked me if I knew anything about you or Nas?" I wrinkled my eyebrows at her, dreading what was about to come from her mouth next.

"I remember."

"I did mention something to them. It was nothing about you, but I told them about Nas. I let them know as much as I could about him and that day he left, I described him to the police, and I even sent Serena outside to get the license plate number of the car he drove away in."

Suddenly, my mind went back to that day. The argument we had outside right before he left when it was beginning to rain. I remembered Serena coming outside to check on me and then, it all started to click. The fact that, even though he denied it, I know Nas sent somebody over there to kill Stacey, and there wasn't doubt in my mind that he was behind Allen's murder. All of that, added to the fact that Nas was arrested around the same time, painted a crystal-clear picture in my mind. Everything was coming together from my point of view but at the same time, I felt like Stacey brought it on her. If she never said anything, then she wouldn't have gotten Nas's attention. I don't know if the police began to sweat him shortly after he left Stacey's house or what, but all I knew was he had a reason to come back at her, and if she had told me before, then she would have been the one that everyone pressed to leave the city.

"Mama, why did you do that? Why did you tell anyone? You lied to me."

Her eyes watered, "I know baby, and I'm sorry. I was just worried about you and Prince. I was worried for your safety, and I figured I could get him away from y'all and keep y'all safe since it seemed like you weren't ever going to leave the city." The tears fell down her face as she began crying. "Now, I realize that I not only put myself in danger, I put my family at risk and I got Allen killed! It's my fault! It's all my fault!" she said as she began to cry inconsolably. I could relate to her pain more than she thought because I felt like I was the reason Uncle Stew had gotten strung out again and even worse, the reason the Prince had gotten kidnapped. I reached for her and held her in my arms as she let every bit of her pain out in the form of tears. Prince was still sound asleep through it all, and the strength of her cries started to cause tears of my own. "Mama," I said, trying to calm her, "it's alright. It's going to be okay." She released me,

"No, it's not, Lyric. Serena called me earlier this morning and told me that there has been a guy asking for me at the house. She said he comes around once every other day, and he has been for the past few days."

"A guy?"

She wiped her tears, "Yes. Some guy. She is not at home alone; she has a handful of her cousins with her, but she says she felt unsafe even though she had her gun. He just had all of these bad vibes coming from him, so I just told her to come out here."

"Is she coming?"

"Yes. She packed up a few things and said she is on her way."

I thought about Vinny in the same light, knowing that the weird things he was experiencing at Big Mama's house were probably related to the guy that was looking for Stacey. The only thing I could hope is that she wasn't being trailed on the way out here. In the dream I had earlier, Nas knew exactly where I lived out here and even though it was a dream, I knew that pieces of reality were scattered throughout. Stacey calmed down and wiped her eyes,

"I'm sorry for this, Lyric. Had I just kept my damn mouth shut maybe you guys would still be able to live in Milwaukee. He probably thinks you told the police to get the heat off you or something, but even more, my family would be safe, and my husband would still be alive."

"Don't put all of that on yourself, Mom. Don't, okay? Things happen. Nas is just—"

"He is just the one that killed his own father and is trying to kill his own mother and sister. That is what Nas is, and just to think that I gave birth to my husband's murderer is sickening in itself! I gave birth to the man that is now threatening my family and has been a menace to society. That came out of me, Lyric. Me!"

She yelled as her sadness quickly turned to anger. Her fists balled up, and a scowl appeared on her face as she sat in front of me, motionless. Just then, Prince opened his eyes and coughed, and as she turned to look at him her anger began to subside. She picked him up and held him in her arms and immediately, I realized that I was not the only one Prince had the ability to cool; he had that same effect on his grandmother. "Are you going to be alright?" I asked her as she held onto him. She shook her head yes, and I reached over and kissed both of them before I headed back downstairs.

I glanced out the front room window just to make sure everything was normal. The orange-ish colored sun was sending its last rays across the city, and a group of children were headed to the pool with beach towels and balls in their hands. They weren't as loud as the kids on Big Mama's block were, and if I didn't see them, I wouldn't have even noticed that they were out there. My phone rang seconds later. The number wasn't saved in my phone, but I answered it anyway,

"Hello?"

"This Lyric?"

"Who is this?"

"It's Malley. I wanted to talk to you for a minute."

"About what?"

"Business."

It was at that moment that I saw things differently with her. I knew what type of operation she ran, but I also knew what else it meant for me. Nas was coming one way or the other, and I had to handle it the best way I could.

"Aight," I replied, "we can talk."

Chapter 6

I met her just down the street from my apartment at a small, mom-and-pop burger joint. When I walked inside, she had already taken a seat in the corner of the restaurant.

"Whassup Malley?"

Her fire red hair seemed to glow while it was pulled back in a ponytail. Her full lips were heavily coated with lip gloss, and she winked at me when I took a seat next to her.

"Hey, Lyric. It's good to see you. I was thinking you weren't gonna come through."

"Nah, I don't have a reason not to. You're good people from what I can see."

"Cool."

The waitress came over to us, "Can I get you, ladies, anything?" Malley looked at me,

"You hungry?"

"I'm straight. I'll just take a sprite."

"Well, fuck what she's saying, I'm hungry. Let me get a bacon cheeseburger with fries and a coke."

"Okay. I'll have that right out."

The waitress walked away as Malley kept her eyes on her ass, "Damn, white girl was kind of thick, wasn't she?" I looked in her direction while I could still see her. She was, and it caused me to think about the times I had with Keyonna before I killed Big Tuck. Malley snapped me out of it before I could think any further.

"So, you working again? You know you lit that store on fire with yo' words that day you left."

"Shit, I had to get out of that bitch. That chick was too much to deal with on a daily."

"I feel you. I could tell she was an asshole when she walked over there."

"Yeah, she was."

"So, you're not working?"

"Nah."

She scooted closer to me, "Why don't you stop fucking around and come with us. I'm telling you, you will make at least a couple thousand each night you come out with us. Easy money. Easy fucking money, Lyric." She didn't know that I had already committed to doing that in my mind. This operation she had going on was something I could use to my advantage in more than a few ways, especially since I knew Nas had to be dealt with.

"I don't know, I mean, I'm not trying to get into too much trouble out here. That's the whole reason I left Milwaukee."

"Milwaukee?" she said with a blank expression on her face, "you lived in Milwaukee?"

"Yeah, why?"

Her eyes drifted off to my right as if some memory completely took over her mind. Her eyelashes extended far beyond the lids of her eyes and just as I was in the middle of my admiration of them, the waitress came back and placed our drinks on the table. Malley looked at her as she smiled and walked away from us again. I spoke up,

"Malley, what's up with Milwaukee?"

"Oh," she shook her head, "it's just, a nigga I used to fuck with moved to Milwaukee a few years ago. He was fine as hell. Cute, nice body, he even had dimples and shit, but he was a thug ass nigga that produced and sold drugs. Nobody would have guessed it just by looking at him, though, he just didn't have that type of aura, you know? He was actually making a lot of money both ways, but he just decided to stick with the drug shit over the music."

Nas? I thought to myself, wanting her to continue but she stopped. "Oh," I said, pushing her along, "I used to talk to a nigga like that, but I couldn't fuck with him anymore. That drug shit wasn't my thing, you know?" She smiled, "I feel you; it wasn't mine either, but the nigga just hooked me in and shit. One minute, we were lovely dovely but the next the nigga just flipped on me."

"He flipped on you?"

"Started treating me like shit. It is part of the reason, well, the only reason I don't fuck with niggas anymore. I mean, I fuck with them sometimes because I need a real dick every now and then, but that's it. I don't fuck with them as far as relationships and shit go."

I took a sip of my soda and kept prodding for information,

"I feel you. I'm kind of in the same boat. The nigga I was fucking with did me wrong, too. I mean, it wasn't as severe as you or nothing. The nigga I fucked with was just a nickel and dime hustler, you know? He wasn't a kingpin or nothing."

"Well," she said as she ran her finger around the top of her glass, "this nigga was a kingpin back in Ohio. Like I said, shit was going well until he flipped. The nigga," she paused. It seemed as if she recollected some memory that was just too painful to bring up again. "He poisoned me." She clenched a knife in her hand, and it began to shake. "That bitch ass nigga poisoned me, and he will get his and trust me, that bitch ass nigga is going to die, and it won't be by anything but my own fuckin' hands."

The waitress came back and placed Malley's food on the table and with that, she loosened the knife that was clenched in her hand. She relaxed and let the waitress know she appreciated her service.

"That bitch is beautiful," she said as she placed a few fries in her mouth. She turned towards me, "I mean, she ain't cuter than you or nothin' like that, but she fine as hell in an everyday kind of way. You sure you don't want nothing to eat?"

"Yeah, I'm sure."

She ate a few more fries. "But back to the topic, you should really fuck with us. Like I said, we can use somebody like you."

I took another sip of my soda as she dug into her food. I already made the decision in my mind; I just didn't want to seem anxious by accepting what she was saying so quickly. She spoke in-between bites of her burger as I gave off hints that I was paying attention but my mind was clearly somewhere else. The man she described reminded me exactly of Nas. The way things were good in the beginning and then they suddenly flipped out of nowhere, and even the way she described his appearance was similar, not to mention he was doing his thing in Ohio before he came to Milwaukee. If I had to guess, she just described Nas, but I didn't think that now was the time to tell her. It was too early, and I had to figure some more things out before I rushed into that. This was a game of chess, and if you move too quickly without thinking then the shit is going to be over before you begin, so I just let it simmer for now. The one thing that stood out to me was that she said he poisoned her. I remembered when I went to jail that he said I was going to die a slow death and even in the dream, the same sentiments were echoed. I wanted to know what that poison was because chances are, if she was poisoned then I would be too.

Chapter 7

For the next few weeks, I hung out with Malley so I could get a better idea of who she was. That was my purpose for it all, but hers was entirely different. I think she was feeling me in a sexual way, and she wasn't shy about flirting. From smacking me on my ass when I walked by to stroking my hair when I was next to her, she did it all and everything in between. I was horny as fuck, though, so it really came down to whatever we wanted to do. There wasn't a man that caught my attention in Rockwall, and the ones that did were either too young or they were too feminine. To me, there weren't many things much worse than a man who wore clothing tighter than a female or one who was too tied up in their own emotions. That was one of the main reasons I stayed away from so many bitches my whole life, so the last thing I wanted to see in a man were female characteristics.

The times that Malley could have fucked, she pulled back. "Nah baby, I want to but I can't. Not right now." That was her response and after a few times I just started to believe she was a tease, but Quandra told me that wasn't the case because she had fucked other chicks inside their operation before. Even with that, I knew there was something else up with her, but I just couldn't put my finger on it. Stacey decided to stay out in Rockwall with me a little longer and a day after she told me the shit that she did to Nas, Serena showed up with a few bags of her own. I made sure nobody followed her out here, and she said she had made a few stops before she came here because she was thinking the same way I was. I could tell she was a little shaken up about everything, but now she could at least rest easy for a little while. I thought it was funny how all of the people that said I should move out of Milwaukee ended up being the ones that would follow me out. All except Vinny. I'd talked to him a few times since he visited and he kept telling me he was all right when I tried to get him to come back out here for a while.

"Vinny, bruh, come on man. Just come out here and chill for a minute. At least until we get that shit with Nas situated."

"Nah, fam, I'm good. I'ma come visit y'all again in a minute."

Maybe I picked on him a little too much whenever I noticed him getting soft around me and that made him act like something he wasn't. I laughed though because he and Cedrick were so much alike that I could've sworn they had the same parents, but I respected what he wanted and left him alone. Prince was growing like any other child his age would. He cried out for his dad from time to time and those moments were as hard for me as they were for him. I didn't want to bring him up without his father around, but I knew it was inevitable, especially with the type of life that Nas lived. He could wind up dead or in prison at a moment's notice, but I had always hoped for the best. I never would've thought it would come to this, though. Both of us at odds with each other and that was putting it lightly. As far as I knew, he wanted me dead, and I was beginning to think that his death was the only thing that would guarantee my life. It is the main reason why I decided to get involved with Malley. I knew she had weapons and the one man in the world she may have hated the most was the one person I needed to get rid of. Knowing that, I still played the game slowly, feeling her out as much as I could before I told her the news of us fucking the same nigga. She didn't seem like the jealous type but with a hot head like her, shit could go from zero to one-hundred in the blink of an eye and right now, I didn't have what I needed if it did. I had to play it as cool as possible.

"Aight Lyric, shit, you been kickin' with me long enough. I guess you are feeling me out, and I respect that. I know you're a boss bitch yourself, just like me, so I get it. I understand where you at and where you wanna be, so I'm thinking we come in and run this shit together. From what Quandra was telling me, you already had some shit going on in Milwaukee."

"Quandra told you? What she tell you?"

Her eyes widened as she began laughing. "Calm down, baby girl, she just told me how you had niggas scared of you back in yo' city and shit, that's all. She didn't give me any details; she just told me that if you were behind me that I didn't have anything to worry about because you weren't worried about poppin' niggas if it came to it."

She leaned back on my couch and crossed her leg one over the other, exposing a tattooed portion of her thigh. That was just one of the many that decorated her body, but the one right between her breasts was what I loved. They were cat prints, similar to what Eve had tattooed on her chest. The prints went from the middle of her breasts and trailed down her side, stopping just before her pussy. I licked the entire path, and just when I was headed to her box, she stopped me. No matter what I did or how horny I was she just never let it go that far.

As Malley and I got closer, some of the chicks in the group started showing their jealousy. From what I heard, Quandra said that most of the new girls that came in got fucked as a part of their initiation. She said when I first came in Malley wanted to but for some reason, she didn't go through with it. I remembered that time like it just happened a few days ago. The other chicks didn't like the fact that I was being favored out of everyone, but they couldn't do shit about it. Malley would have beat the shit out of them, killed them, or just got rid of them some other way. If she didn't do it, I would have. It was odd though because she wasn't as ruthless as Nas, but suddenly I felt that we were developing the same sort of relationship, except this time, I wasn't behind anyone. I was becoming the forefront of the operation, and I didn't want anything else.

I parked in the same spot I did when I first arrived at the apartment complex. A few guys were gathered around a truck, talking with each other as I watched them from a short distance. They all had locked hair, jeans, and v-neck white t-shirts on as they puffed and blew smoke into the air. I immediately thought about Nas as I observed them from my seat. Physically, I couldn't tell them apart from the dope boys that he had hustling out on the corners. They laughed with each other, chrome pistols glimmering under the streetlight whenever their positions exposed it on their waists. From what I heard, Nas was still in prison and the charges he went in on were building. I didn't know how much of what I heard was true, but I knew he was still in there. I got out of the car as the guys suddenly turned to look at me. "Daamn," one of them yelled out as I headed to the apartment. Just then, the same one that yelled out walked over to me.

"Whassup, Lil' Mama?"

"Nothing."

I kept walking, but he was persistent,

"Can I talk to you?"

"You already are."

"I'm sayin', though, can you stop for a minute so I can talk to you?"

"I got somewhere to be."

He reached out and grabbed my arm, but I jerked away from him,

"Don't touch me, aight?"

A straight-faced glare blazed from his eyes. I could tell he didn't have the patience, but neither did I.

"What the fuck is wrong with you?"

"I don't need you puttin' yo' hands on me, that's what's wrong with me."

The guys he stood around with began walking over in our direction as he gave me a disturbing smile,

"Look, I can tell you're not from around here but around here, bitches don't talk any kind of way to me."

"And, nigga? Who are you?"

He laughed, then reached down and smacked my ass. In turn, I balled my fist and jabbed him in his mouth. I heard two guns load bullets into their chambers, and as soon as I looked over, they were aimed right at me. The guy I jabbed in the mouth spit out a little blood onto the cement and turned to look at me. Just as he approached, Malley yelled from the top of the stairs, "Deeko, back the fuck up," she said, leaning over the banister. Deeko looked up to her and said,

"Nah, Malley, you need to control this bitch. She apparently doesn't know how shit goes around here."

"Whatever way you think it's going with me, it's not. So you can chill all that bullshit."

Malley came down the stairs and stood between us, "Deeko, take ya' ass on," she said, daring him to step any closer. "We'll take care of this shit later," he replied as he turned and left, his guys following along with him. Malley turned back to me, "I can handle myself," I said, peering back at her while keeping Deeko in my line of sight. "I know you can, but that's not the point here. Come on, I'll talk to you a little more inside."

We walked into the apartment as a few women loaded clips into pistols and placed them on the tables they were sitting at. They were all dressed in skimpy clothing with makeup flawlessly painted on their faces. A few of them acknowledged me as Malley took me to the back room and shut the door. "Deeko is security," she explained, "and he is paid with pussy." I folded my arms and leaned against the dresser.

"So, you fuck that nigga for his protection?"

"Me? Hell naw. I don't fuck with niggas no more. It's bitches here that we kick a lil' dust, and whenever they want to fuck, we send one of them out."

"So, you're their pimp?"

She laughed, "Shit, I didn't even think about it until now. I guess I am. But anyways, he just thought you were a new girl because his fool ass has been begging for some new pussy and I told him I would get him some."

"He had the wrong one."

She walked closer to me, brushing her breasts against mine, "Absolutely. He had the wrong fucking one."

She licked her lips and ran her finger from my shoulder to the middle of my arm. I wasn't even uncomfortable with her doing it. In fact, I was beginning to welcome it, and I don't even know how or why. Maybe it was because with the last two men I was with one ended up getting murdered and the other turned out to be everything I thought he wasn't. It could have been the fact that I'd been around so many guys, and I knew that most of them were full of shit. Whatever it was, I didn't feel it with Malley, and she could tell. She moved in closer and kissed me on my lips and gripped a handful of my ass with her hand. I smiled, and suddenly, the door burst open. Quandra just stood there as Malley switched her attention to her,

"Damn, Quandra, don't you know how to knock?"

"My bad, Malley. I was just letting you know that the niggas are at the spot. They ready for us. What up, Lyric?"

"Shit."

"Aight, well y'all get ready to ride out then. I'll be out there in a minute."

Quandra closed the door, and Malley walked over to the drawer and pulled out two pistols. She extended one towards me but I said, "Nah, I'm good." She looked confused,

"You good? Yeah, I know you're good, but this is just in case." I reached into my purse and pulled out an all-black .357. Her eyes widened, "Damn. Ok, I see you, Miss Lyric," she said, sliding one of the pistols back in the drawer. "You are definitely ready. Let's go," she said, walking out of the room before me. The front room was clear when we walked out and headed down to the truck. I saw Deeko standing back in the same spot he and his boys stood when I pulled up. He glared at me, and I returned it right back to him; I don't know who he thought I was, but I had a feeling he was going to find soon out.

We pulled up to a hotel on the outskirts of downtown Rockwall. It was away from the regular hustle and bustle of the small city as the darkness loomed in the skies above us. It was six women, including Malley and me, and we were all dressed in the appropriate attire. Tight clothing, short skirts, and skimpy tops but everything was concealed under long, trench coats. Malley gathered us all together to give a rundown of how everything was going to go,

"Listen. We got to dance for a little bit and get them niggas nice and hard. Now, if you fuck or you want to fuck, then give the sign, and we will hold off. If nobody gives the sign, then I'll move in on them when the time is right. Anybody got any shit they wanna say? Speak now or forever hold your peace." She glanced around the small circle, and there were no objections. "Aight," she said, "let's go."

The men were waiting for us in their room on the fourth floor. There were three of them, one overweight and anxious to see us, the other two were slim with short haircuts. The overweight man sat on the bed while the other two positioned themselves near the lone desk that sat in the cheap hotel room. I looked around, knowing that I would never set foot in a place like this on my own, let alone lay down on the bed. The carpet was stained and had begun to roll up from the corners. The walls were dingy and decorated with different types of odd-colored markings, looking as if something had exploded in the room. "It's about time y'all showed up," the obese man said as he scooted forward onto the bed, "y'all was supposed to be here an hour ago." Malley walked towards him, bending down as her titties swayed back and forth right in his face, "I'm sorry, sweetheart, but I guarantee you that good things come to those who wait," she ran her finger across his chest, "and I will definitely have a surprise for you before it is all said and done." An annoying smile bolted across his face, and his slightly put-out attitude suddenly shifted into joy.

Malley stood up and winked towards us and two by two the girls went into the bathroom to get ready. As they went in, the other girls entertained the men, flirting with them and caressing every part of their bodies to get them willing to be finessed. It was a rush to watch it all unfolding before my eyes, to know that one side of the room is expecting one thing, but the other end of the room was going to give them the exact opposite. Malley walked over to me and whispered into my ear, "Just sit back and watch this shit. This is why I don't fuck with niggas anymore, they are so fucking stupid," she said, winking at me. She turned back around just as two girls stepped out of the bathroom with nothing on but their bras and a g-string. They clapped their asses together almost in sync as they switched places with two of the other women. Before I knew it, they were all barely clothed and ready to entertain. One of the men looked over at me, "Why she ain't getting dressed? I wanna see her ass, too," he said, demanding that I participate. Malley began to speak, but I stopped her, "Nah, it's cool," I stated with a smile, "I'll give him what he wants."

I went to the bathroom and stripped down naked, leaving nothing on except the coat I wore into the hotel. When I came outside, the girls had already begun going to work with the music on in the background. It wasn't loud enough to attract attention, but it was at a volume just right for the room. Malley mounted the overweight man and ground slowly on him in a reverse cowgirl position, clapping her ass as he smacked dollar bills onto her behind. "Nah, nigga," one of the girls said, "we don't fuck with one dollar bills. Y'all said y'all were some ballers, drop the twenties or we are gone." The men quickly pulled rolls of money out of their pockets and with that, the women began dancing again. I walked over to the man that demanded my attention and straddled him as he sat in the desk chair. "You wanted me," I whispered to him, his gold-toothed grill exposed as he smiled back at me. "Hell yeah," he said, clutching my ass in both of his hands. I smiled, "Alright. I'm here, so what do you want to do?" I asked, reaching down to unbuckle his pants as he tossed the twenties at me. "Let me slide it in," he replied, silently begging me with his eyes. I reached down and pulled his dick out of his pants once I loosened his belt. He grinned. "Hell yeah," he said, tossing more twenties at me.

I glanced over at Malley as she made a gun signal with her hand. I figured that was the sign because two of the women went towards the bags. With that, I got up off of him, his dick still exposed for everyone to see. Malley walked to her purse and pulled out her pistol. When she cocked it, she spun around and immediately the pleasuring smile that was on her face was replaced with a heartless scowl. She aimed the pistol directly at the man she was on top of a minute ago, "Where is the rest of it!?" she demanded. The fat man laughed, "Oh shit, you've gotta be fuckin' shittin' me!" The two other men tried to pull their pants up, but three more pistols were pointed in their direction, and they froze in place, their once erect penises immediately lost the firmness. "Nah, this ain't no game. Now where the fuck is it!?" The man I was on top of yelled out, "Fuck this shit, bitch. I ain't givin' y'all shit. Y'all gon' have to kill me first." I walked over to my purse and grabbed my pistol. "Shit, you strapped, too?" he said as I walked back over to him. Suddenly, I lifted the gun into the air and cracked him in the face with it as hard as I could. "Nah, nigga. We won't kill you. We'll make sure you feel as much pain as fuckin' possible before we would even think about killin' you. Now, you wanna tell us where the bread is, or are you trying to get smacked again?" He gripped the side of his face as blood began to trickle from his eyebrow. "Pete," he said, writhing in pain, "just give them the shit, nigga. Fuck!" I smiled and leaned in towards him, "You should be careful what you ask for."

"That's a good idea… Pete," Malley said with a smile on her face, "you should take ya man's advice. We want all the shit. Cell phones, money, jewelry. All of it! And hurry up!" Pete slowly walked over to a black bag in the closet, glancing back and forth at the guns as if he was sizing up the collateral damage if he made a move. Three guns were pointed directly at him as he moved. "If you feel like being a hero, go ahead. Smith and Wesson will end all that shit in a hurry," one of the girls said, causing him to think twice about whatever was going through his mind.

With that, he sighed and reached for the bag inside the closet and tossed it to Malley. Malley pulled it open and sifted through it. She smiled as if she was pleased with the turnout. "Alright ladies," she said, "We can roll." We grabbed our things, making sure to take away their jewelry and cell phones before we left. I was surprised when they didn't come out the room after us. They didn't seem like the type that would try to retaliate or anything, but as I rode back with Malley in the car, I couldn't help but see the holes in this operation. I knew how to come in and make things run smoother. All it would have taken is one slip up, and those niggas could have killed one or two of us before we even had the chance to get out.

Malley sped away while the other car followed behind her. "Shit, we got at least 25 stacks. I told them to bring that, and we would dance and fuck all night," she said, laughing to herself. I remained quiet as she peered over at me and said,

"Lyric? I said 25 stacks."

"I heard you."

"That shit don't excite you?"

"I mean, I've held 25 stacks before, so it's really nothing new to me right now. I was just thinking about some other shit."

"What other shit?"

"How you can make this thing run a lot smoother. Like, I think the niggas should be tied up, for one. They could have had pistols hidden anywhere in that room and got to it, maybe even got a couple shots off before we could. I mean, that's just something that needs to be fixed because these bitches might mess around and get shot."

"Oh?" she said, looking at me as if I offended her. "You got anything else to say?"

"Yeah. One of those bitches weren't ready for that shit. I could see it in her eyes, and if she had to pull the trigger, she would have frozen up. I knew it when I saw her pull out. You can just tell certain shit about people sometimes."

"Who?"

"The bitch that had the pink shit on."

"Aight," she said, looking into the rearview mirror, "I had a feeling about her, but I just wasn't sure. She told me she was straight, so I left her alone."

"She ain't straight at all. She's going to fuck around and get somebody killed in the end. She ain't ready for this shit."

The car ride back to the apartment was quiet. I wasn't sure if she was taking what I said with a grain of salt or if I was just altogether pissing her off. I knew I could help, though; it was like I was born to do this kind of shit. Finessing niggas like this never crossed my mind though and if I had, I would've been the bitch that Malley thought she was. Not only that, I would be better at it. Without a shadow of a doubt.

Chapter 8

It didn't take long for me to come in and help the operation flow smoother. I told them that we needed to hit a few spots in the city and then lay low for a while. When we went in, we had to look completely different from what we usually looked like. Weave, short haircuts, makeup and everything else had to be different. All of that shit could make a female so indistinguishable from one day to the next that it would be nearly impossible to identify her. That's what we had to do, and I was surprised that they hadn't thought of it in the beginning. They usually hopped from city to city, finessing niggas that way but I didn't have time to travel all around like that. I had a son that I had to keep an eye on and a baby daddy that I felt wanted both of us dead, and the moment he got the opportunity he was going to take advantage of it. I didn't want that to happen, so I knew I had to stay as close as I could. The money was rolling in hand over hand. We usually did the shit late night, so whenever I left the house, I knew Stacey would be curious about it all, but thankfully she never said anything. She gave me a strange look all the time but she still respected me as an adult, and I appreciated it. I knew that if Big Mama was here, she would be all up my ass with questions about where I was headed, especially since Prince was getting bigger. I laughed as I heard her threats echo inside my mind.

I got to Malley's spot later that night. Deeko was outside as soon as I parked and ever since the first night that we bumped heads, he didn't say anything to me at all. He peered at me with a cold, hard look on his face but I glared at him the same way. The pistols I took from Malley's spot were always around me, and I didn't have a problem pulling out on him. As a matter a fact, I'm pretty sure that between us, I would have been the first one to fire shots.

There were only a handful of chicks inside when I walked through the door. Quandra was directing a couple new faces on what to do and where to go once we got inside. "Whassup, Lyric," she said while the other chicks looked in my direction.

"Hey, Quandra. New people?"

"Hell yeah. They ready, though."

I scanned through them, and my eyes locked when they landed on one girl in particular. I walked over to her and yanked her up by the arm, "What the fuck you doing here, Alisha?" She laughed and pulled her arm out of my grasp, "I was wondering if you were going to recognize me. I'm here the same reason you are. I'm tryna get paid, and a bitch as thick as I am? Shit, this is EASY money, Lyric. You ain't the only one with a fat ass and nice titties." Quandra walked up to us, smiling, "She bad, ain't she? These old, crusty ass niggas love them young hoes. They're ready to fucking give them everything they got, especially this one. This hoe right here actually sucked a nigga's dick so good that we tied the nigga up and robbed him and he didn't even realize the shit was happening until she stopped." Alisha smiled, proud of what her work as Quandra continued, "She is a fuckin' star in the making."

I peered at Quandra,

"Quandra, this bitch ain't even 17 yet."

"Oh my God, Lyric, so the fuck what? I mean, you trying to say that because she is still 16 that it is the straw that breaks the camel's back? I mean, out of all the fucked up shit we are doing, you have a problem with this the most?"

"She young, Quandra! She got her whole fuckin' life ahead of her. We mid-twenties and older in here, you know what I'm sayin?"

Alisha spoke up, "Look, I don't see my mama in here and ain't neither one of y'all my guardian. I'm here cuz I want to make money so fuck all the bullshit, aight Lyric? I'm here, the money is there, and I know these thirsty niggas want some of this young pussy, so fuck it. Let's get paid together."

I stepped closer to Quandra, "Fuck that. Quandra, why the fuck you bring her out here!?"

Quandra laughed, more as a warning to me than out of humor, "Lyric, I'ma tell you this once, aight? Don't put yo' fuckin' hand in my face no more." The smile on her face suddenly went away. "Or what, Quandra? What? You gon' get yo' ass beat again like we outside of George Webb? What the fuck are you going to do, Quandra?" Just then, Malley walked into the front room in nothing but her bra and some boy shorts, "What the fuck is goin on? Damn! I'm trying to fuckin' chill before we get this bread and y'all muthafuckas in here blowing my high and shit. What the fuck?"

Quandra peered at me for a few moments before she turned away and walked back to the table, "Nothin, Malley. Everything straight. I'm just going over shit with them before we roll out." Malley looked at me, "Lyric?" I glared at Quandra for an instant and then answered Malley, "I'm good." I shook my head at Alisha and then walked to the back of the apartment as Malley followed behind me. I sat on the bed, and she closed the door behind her and straddled me, "You aight?" I took the blunt from her and inhaled the marijuana.

"I'm straight. Why are you lettin' these young bitches in here, though? Sixteen? They are not ready for this kind of shit."

She leaned in and kissed me slowly on the lips, "Lyric, they ready. I wouldn't even let them in here if they weren't. That chick out there, though? She is a fucking pro and even if they fuck up with us, then them niggas doing security need pussy. Shit, they can contribute in some kind of way if they are not going in with us." I looked out the window as I took another drag on the blunt. She put her hand on my cheeks and turned my attention back towards her, "Whassup with that lil' bitch out there, though? You know her or something?" I passed the blunt back to her before I answered,

"I used to work with her, that's all."

"At the grocery store when you snapped on that fat bitch?"

"Yeah."

"Look, she came in here, and she was ready to work off the top. She fucked one of the niggas out there, and when he told me how she got down, I let her get a run with us. Shit, her execution was flawless, Lyric. She knows what she doing so let that chick make us some more money. I mean, you there. I'm there. Ain't shit going to happen to her, aight?"

She leaned in to kiss me again, pressing her lips softly against mine. "Aight," I said, "but get the fuck off me, though, I don't have time for you to be teasing me right now." She laughed, "We are going to get it on, baby. Trust me on that."

A little while later, we headed to the east side of Rockwall. Quandra ran into a guy in that area as she was shopping for some clothes and started talking to him. She found out what kind of car he drove and when she saw that it was his, she laid the bait for him, and he took it without thinking twice. We didn't usually make house calls because I wanted to make sure that we were in complete control of the situation. Houses were generally out of the question because there were too many things that could go wrong, but by the way Quandra described the guy, he was a complete square and hadn't done anything bad a day in his life. When we saw him, my fear of anything happening that we couldn't control was gone.

He was tall and bony with a neat haircut and skinny glasses. He stood on his porch with his hands in his pockets waiting for us when we arrived. A silly, goofy ass grin stretched across his face the closer we got to him. "H...hi," he said, stuttering through his words, "my name is Austin. Nice to see you again, Quandra." Quandra smiled and gave him a hug, then introduced the rest of us. Just after that, he led us into his home. The inside looked much better than the outside. The living room was large enough to hold two of mine inside of it. The couches were large with fluffy pillows across the seats. The carpet was gray and plush, the type that your feet would sink right into as soon as you took your shoes off. The dining area was decorated with crystal plates and glass cups on top of a marble-colored table. Suddenly, four men walked out of the kitchen and into the room where we stood. They all resembled Austin; tall and nerdy, the type who haven't been around a woman in years. I could tell this was going to be easy money. "Um, can you show me to your bathroom?" I asked Austin.

He led me down a hallway and pointed me in the direction I needed to go. "Thank you," I said. He nervously lowered his head and smiled before he walked away. As soon as he was out of the hall, I began to scan the other rooms. All of the doors were unlocked. Three bedrooms in this hallway and one bathroom—they were empty. I crept upstairs to find another bathroom and two more bedrooms, much larger than the ones that were downstairs. It looked as if this was his parents' house and he lived at home with them. I didn't care because either way, they had bread and it was going to be with us before the end of the night. I searched for cameras and anything else that would make our night harder than it should be and when everything cleared, I made my way back downstairs. Austin tapped his foot on the ground with his arms crossed,

"You can't just go walking through my home like that."

"I'm sorry, baby," I said, smiling, "I just had to check out your house. I haven't been in any home this big before."

I walked over to him and rubbed my hand against his dick. Immediately, I felt the blood rush to it, and he backed away from me with a nervous smile on his face. I stepped in closer to him, took his hand and put it on my ass, "Do you forgive me?" I asked as seductively as I could. He fixed his glasses and backed up a little more, "I do. It's… it's all right," he said, his face reddening by the second. "Good, now come with me," I responded as I led him back to the front room and sat him on the couch near the rest of his friends. I walked over to Malley and winked at her, giving her the sign that everything was clear. The other chicks were dressed down and ready to start, and with that, Malley turned on the music and the party started.

Alisha licked her lips before she headed towards one of the men and looked at me, "Watch this," she said confidently as she switched her ass back and forth until she got to one of the men on the couch. When she was just a few feet in front of him, she did a handstand and came down with her crotch right on top of his and then pulled herself up until she was face-to-face with him. She grabbed his head and pushed it down into her chest as she began grinding on him. She moved up and down and then suddenly, pushed herself back down to the floor and put her face near his zipper. I stood back and watched him as he smiled, his face turning just as red as Austin's when I put his hand on my behind.

She pulled his zipper down and reached inside his pants. He tried to stop her, but she smacked his hands away and kept going for it. When she pulled out his dick, it was bigger than I expected it to be. I think it even caught Alisha by surprise as a devilish grin flashed across her face. She turned to look at Malley and gave her the sign that she wanted to fuck. With that, we all knew that we had to wait until she was done before any of us robbed the men. She spun around and bent over in front of him, shaking her ass back and forth as his dick shot straight up in the air. Just then, she eased her way down onto him, "Wait," he said, nervously reaching inside his pocket for a condom. Alisha turned around and snatched it out of his hand, rolling it onto his dick with her mouth. She sucked him slowly for a few moments and then spun back around and eased down on top of him. Her titties bounced in the air as she got into it more and right next to him, another chick began fucking the man she was dancing for.

The moans seemed to drown out the music as the two women fucked and screamed out in pain and pleasure while they were on top of them. "Oh my god," Alisha yelled out, "fuuuuuck!" She gripped the edge of the couch as Austin held onto her hips and started pounding her even harder. Malley stood in the corner, playing with herself as she watched the two of them fuck in front of her. Sometimes, it went like this. The chicks would end up fucking longer than expected and we would just sit there and wait until they were finished. It made it easier to rob them afterward though because they would literally be too tired to do anything else and we took advantage of it.

When the two chicks were done they got up, and Malley turned off the music. Right after that, we both pulled out the pistols as Austin and his friend's pants were still down. The other two men were sitting on the floor with their backs against the wall. Austin yelled out, "Hey, hey, what... what are you guys doing?!" I directed two of the women to go upstairs and search the bedrooms. The other two chicks searched the rooms at the bottom. When one of them came back, she said there was a safe upstairs. I walked over to Austin,

"Hey baby," I said with the gun pointed directly at him, "you want to tell me the combination to the safe?"

"No! No, I don't!"

I laughed and flipped my gun around, "Now see, I'm going to ask you again. If you happen to say no, I'm going to take the handle of this gun and smash it into your fuckin' balls. Now, you have a pretty nice size dick, and I would hate for that to go to waste because you can't use it anymore. I'm sure getting smacked down there with this pistol a few times will fuck all that shit up for you, don't you think?"

Sweat beads began to appear on his forehead, but he remained silent. "Well, alright," I said as I lifted the gun into the air. "Waaaait! 2-5-7-8, 2-5-7-8!" he yelled out at the top of his lungs. I looked towards Quandra, and she was already headed back up the stairs. She came back down with a handful of diamonds and a couple stacks of hundred dollar bills. I smiled at Austin, "Cool. Now, that wasn't so hard, was it?" Tears began to roll down his face as he and his friends sat there dejected. "Now," Malley said, "I would hate to find out what happens to the one who snitched. I mean, I don't think you all want that kind of trouble, right?" She pulled out their ID's, "Austin, Bradley, Donald and um, Hank Ferguson?" They all shook their heads no and with that, we tied them up and left the home.

Chapter 9

Both Serena and Stacey were still out in Rockwall with me. Serena's job was able to transfer her out here, so she figured this was going to be a permanent change for her. Surprisingly, she liked the city, but she never did much back in Milwaukee anyway so she wasn't worried about the nightlife. She was good with a bowling alley and a few restaurants to eat out at from time to time, but Stacey was having trouble adjusting. Against our advice, she would go back to Milwaukee from time to time just to check on the house. We both called her almost every hour she was away just to make sure everything was alright with her.

"Girl, if you two don't stop calling my phone, there is going to be a real problem when I get back there!"

She snapped at us, but she knew that we were just concerned. I figured that she would rather us care too much than not care at all. A few days later, I felt myself getting sick. It felt like the flu was coming over me but I brushed it off. The symptoms had been off and on for a few weeks now, so I didn't think much of it. It was more annoying than anything else, but after Stacey kept prodding me, I finally went to get checked out. She said she wouldn't stop bugging me until I did so I took myself to a minute clinic not too far from where I lived.

"Miss Sutton?"

A middle-aged black woman beckoned to me and led me to the back of the office. I sat down, and she pulled up a chair next to me.

"So, what seems to be the problem? You're just feeling a little sick?"

"Yeah, off and on for the past few weeks."

"Really?" she straightened her glasses as she glared down at a paper I filled out when I came in, "what are your symptoms?"

"A runny nose, sore throat, stomach ache, and a headache from time to time."

"Do you feel tired?"

"Yeah, but it's not too bad."

"Hm," she glanced back up at me, "have you gotten a flu shot?"

"No, ma'am."

"It sounds like flu symptoms to me. When was the last time you had a checkup?"

"Um, I really don't know. I honestly haven't been to the doctor in a while."

"Really?" she smiled, "now, Miss Sutton, you can't live your life that way. Something could be wrong with you, and you'd never know. You are a beautiful young woman, but honestly, high blood pressure and kidney failure are silent killers and it is best to know if you have any of those things so you can get a hold of it before it is too late. Do you know if there is a history of high blood pressure or anything like that in your family?"

"I'm not sure. My grandmother had high blood pressure, though."

"Had?"

"Yeah. She passed away almost a year ago."

"Oh," her countenance was dejected, "I'm sorry to hear that."

"I'm sorry to say it."

"How did she die, if you don't mind me asking?"

"Cancer."

"That is tough, and again, I'm sorry for your loss. How about we get you checked out, okay? I mean, just get some blood drawn for starters and we can go from there. Is that alright with you?"

I paused for a moment. As much as I had been through in my life, needles should be the last thing that caused me to be apprehensive, but it was just something about the long end that they stick inside of your arm. Maybe it was because my mother and uncle died with needles in their veins and I didn't want anything to do with them. Now that I think about it, I would have to say that is exactly what it was. The doctor regained my attention,

"Miss Sutton? Is that alright?"

"I have a thing about needles."

She laughed, "Oh, you big baby," she said, tapping me on my knee, "what if I promise you that it'll be over before you know it."

"It's not the pain; it's just the sight of the needle."

She looked to the right momentarily and then turned back towards me, "If that is all it is, I can take care of it, and you will never see a thing."

After a little bit more prodding on her end, I finally gave in to her request. She seemed as if she was concerned and it honestly reminded me of Stacey's persistence. It was one of the things that helped me realize that I was actually cared for and, coming from a woman I had never met before, I couldn't help but feel the same way towards her. She left the room and came back in moments later with a small box and a dark cloth. She sat everything on the table to her right and stared into my eyes,

"Ok, now Miss Sutton."

"You can call me Lyric."

She smiled, "Okay, Lyric. Now, I am going to put this cloth around your eyes, all right?"

I took a deep breath, "Okay."

She tied it around my head, and it made everything around me pitch black. "Now, I just want you to keep still, okay? I'm going to make this as painless as possible." I relaxed in my seat as I felt the bandage tighten around my arm. My heart raced as flashes of my uncle on the ground in the trap house with his eyes open danced through my head. His cold, blank stare stained my thoughts and in moments, tears began flowing from my eyes. I saw my mother in her casket with her arms folded across her chest, just a shell of who she was left for me to see. My mind rewound to her last breaths, and I never saw what positioned she died in, but my imagination had no problem filling in the gaps. She sat on an old, beat up recliner. Pieces of the material were torn off, exposing the white cotton that was packed inside of it. One of the arms was fully exposed, showing the wooden part that held it up. A blue, rubber-like material was tied around her bicep as she put the needle into her vein. Moments later, her head dipped back against the headrest and her hand dropped to her side. Slobber dripped slowly from the corner of her mouth and seconds later, her eyes shut for the very last time.

The doctor took the bandage from around my head, "Okay, we're all finished," she said with a smile. Suddenly, her smile faded as the tears fell solemnly from my eyes. I peered back at her. "Lyric? Did it hurt? What's wrong?" she asked, scooting closer to me. I looked down at the spot where she had stuck the needle into my arm. There was tape wrapped around it with a cotton ball at the point the needle broke my skin. "Lyric? Sweetheart, what is it?" she asked again. I wiped the tears from my eyes and pulled my sleeve back down. "Nothing," I said, "I'm fine. It didn't hurt at all; I was just thinking about some other things." She looked down at my arm and suddenly, it was like she could put the pieces together on her own. I don't know how she could, but she stood up and put her arms around me. I thought it was weird, this woman that I've never met before a day in my life caring for me as if she'd known me since the day I was born.

A few weeks passed when the doctor left a voicemail on my phone,

"Lyric Sutton? Hi, this is Dr. Carter from the minute clinic. We have your results here, but I would like for you to come to my office, not the minute clinic. I want to discuss your results with you, okay? Please contact me as soon as possible."

I came to her office the next day still feeling a little sick but I was used to it by now. I powered through it to the point that the symptoms became a part of me and it was like we learned to coexist together. Dr. Carter called me back to her office a few minutes after I checked in. She hugged me as if she hadn't seen me in years and oddly, I was warmed by it. "So, this is your real office, huh?" I asked as I took my seat. "Yes. I just volunteer at the minute clinic when I can, but this is where I make my money."

There were pictures of her around the room. Some by herself and others with different men, women, and children as if they were one big family. "Are those your kids?" I asked, looking at one of the pictures on her desk. "Children?" she smiled, "No, ma'am. Those are my nieces and my nephew. I don't have any children right now." She looked as if she was saddened by that fact as she continud,

"Yup, I chose to go ahead and get my career together before all of that and it turned out taking longer than I expected. Now, here I am, 41 years old, unmarried and childless."

"Well, if you want, I can let you borrow my boy. He is one, and he is a handful sometimes!"

"Oh, you have a son?" she said. Her face was saddened when the words left her mouth, and it wasn't the response I expected.

"Yes. His name is Prince Jones."

She sighed, "Okay. Well, I think I just need to tell you why I wanted you to come in."

She pulled some papers out of her folder and set them on her table. "Lyric, how long have you been sexually active?" I repositioned myself in my seat and laughed silently to hide some of the embarrassment.

"Why?"

"I'll explain in a moment."

By this time, I was comfortable with her, so I answered, "It's been about seven or eight years now."

"How many partners have you had?"

"Dr. Carter?"

"Trust me, Lyric. It is all for a purpose."

"Okay. Two. Well, three actually."

"Okay." She sighed as she handed me the papers, "There really is no easy way to tell you this, Lyric. You have tested positive for HIV."

I peered at her in disbelief, "What?"

"HIV. Now, before you panic, HIV is not AIDS. It is the virus, and it has the potential for turning into full blown AIDS but as of right now, it is just the virus." She handed me another sheet of paper, "This is a specialized HIV clinic that offers to counsel and things of that nature. I can help you here, but they are much more equipped and can provide you in-depth resources and help for you."

"Wait, what? What are you telling me? I am going to die?"

"No, Lyric," she scooted closer to me and grabbed my hand as my nervousness increased, "Lyric, this is not the end of the world, alright? I want you to understand that—"

"Understand what? You just told me I fucking have HIV. HIV turns into AIDS and AIDS kills people."

My voice began rising, and tears of anger and frustration filled my eyes. Dr. Carter spoke, but I heard nothing come out of her mouth. My life flashed before my eyes. The future I thought I would have with Prince faded away. The life I wanted to live after everything with Nas was taken care of suddenly disappeared, and I was left with images of headstones and funeral services. *This cannot be real*, I thought to myself as I glared at Dr. Carter. Her lips moved as she did her best to console me but I still heard nothing. For a moment, I was deaf, and the only thing that rang out was the heart beating inside my chest. *I am dreaming*, I thought to myself, *come on Lyric, wake up. Wake the fuck up, Lyric!* I waited for my eyes to open just in time to see Prince before he smacked me with one of his toys. I paused to smell the eggs and bacon that Stacey usually cooked in the mornings before I woke up just the way Big Mama had done before she died. I waited and waited, but nothing ever came. Dr. Carter was still in the room with me, speaking and holding onto my hand as her words crashed into my ears as if they were brick walls and fell to the ground. She scooted closer to me and suddenly, her voice pierced through my eardrums just before I blacked out.

I woke up in a bed inside one of the offices. When I opened my eyes, Dr. Carter stood right beside me. "Lyric, are you alright?" There were no tubes or anything in my arm, so I figured I was ok.

"Yeah, I guess so. What happened?"

"You fainted."

"Why? How long have I been here?"

"Just about an hour or so."

"Why did I faint?"

She walked over to the bed where I was laying down and held my hand, "You got some discouraging news about your health, Lyric." Just then, everything came back to my mind. What I had hoped to have been a horrible dream turned out to be a reality. I lowered my head and cried out loud in front of her as she threw her arms around me. I couldn't believe this had happened to me of all people. I never thought I would be one of the ones to experience this, and that is how it always goes. You never believe that it could happen to you, but it did. I was never one to expose my emotions this way, but there was nothing I could do to hold the tears in this time. Everything I was living for no longer mattered. The fact is that I felt I was going to die much sooner than I should have and the worst part about it was that I didn't even know how it happened. *How did it come to this?* I thought to myself as I cried on Dr. Carter's shoulder. This was the beginning of the end for me, and there was nothing I could do to stop it.

Chapter 10

      I took the information from Dr. Carter and drove home about an hour later. Thoughts swirled around in my head and right now, I had no idea how I even contracted the virus. She said that I needed to get Prince tested because it may be a good chance that he contracted it himself depending on when I got it. From her, I found out that the virus could stay dormant for up to ten years before signs of anything showed. In those years, the only people I had sex with were Junie, Nas, and Keyonna and two of those three people were already dead. Immediately, I started to think of Nas. He told me that I was going to die a slow death and that, added to the fact that Malley said that he poisoned her, caused me to point the finger directly at him. "That muthafucka!" I said as my speed slowly increased along with my rage.

      Just then, police lights flashed in my rearview mirror, and I resisted the urge to speed away from him. I pulled to the side, and he got out of the car and walked to the driver's side window. "Do you know how fast you were going?" he asked, straightening out his hat. "No, but you do," I responded, staring directly into his eyes.

"License and insurance, please."

      I handed the items to him and wiped the tear from my eye before it had a chance to fall. It was somewhere between that point and when he gave me my information back that I stopped giving a fuck about everything. He walked back to the car, "Okay, ma'am, I'm just going to let you off with a warning. Make sure you slow down around these parts, I'm sure the next officer won't be as forgiving as I am." I took my things from him and rolled the window up. Moments later, I was gone as he was left standing in the same spot, peering at me as if he regretted not writing me a ticket.

I walked into the door of the apartment as Prince reached for me. I glared at him, ignoring his outstretched hands as Stacey looked at me, "Lyric? What's wrong?" I ignored her and went straight to my room, shutting the door behind me. Moments later, Stacey knocked,

"Lyric? Is everything alright? How did the doctor's go?"

"It was okay."

"Oh, alright. Well, Prince is out here crying for you. Don't you want him?"

"I'll be out there later. I'm just tired right now."

There was a brief pause before she responded, "Okay, Lyric."

I stayed in my room for the rest of the day. When I heard everybody in the house settle down for the night, I left and headed to Malley's apartment. Deeko peered at me as soon as I stepped out of the car. He stood near his apartment with two other guys around him, but today I wasn't with his bullshit. I closed my door and headed in his direction as he folded his arms across his chest. The two guys with him stayed in their spot, and as I walked closer, Deeko spoke out, "The fuck you comin' over here with a full head of steam for? You don't have shit to say to me."

Just then, I took my pistol out and put it to his head, "Look, nigga, I'm sick of you lookin' at me like you got a fuckin' problem every time I come over here. If you got a problem, say it now, nigga? Talk!" He laughed to hide his nervousness, "Look bitch, you got one second to get that fucking gun off me." I took it down to chamber the shot and quickly put it back to his head, "Or what?" His stare was cold. His jawbones gyrated inside his mouth, and his nostrils flared like a small bird spreading its wings for the first time. His boys stood up and pulled their pistols off their waists and chambered bullets.

"You think that shit scares me? If I die now, so be it, but this nigga is coming with me. You ready to die, Deeko?"

"Lyric, what the fuck?!"

I heard Malley's voice from the window, but I didn't take my eyes off Deeko, and he didn't take his eyes off me. The standoff was brief as Quandra ran outside and stood between us. "You betta get this bitch," he said when Quandra stood between us. I pointed the gun just past him and fired a shot right next to his head. He covered his eardrums and bent over, and the two men by his side flinched as if they didn't have pistols in their own hands. "Bitch ass niggas," I said as I put the warm gun back on my waist. I fully expected them to shoot me in my back as I walked away but I couldn't care less. They wouldn't have done anything but took my life for me instead of waiting for a slow ass death on my own.

I walked into the apartment as Malley was on her way to the door with a pistol in her hand. She glanced outside as I kept walking towards the back, ignoring the commotion that was brewing in the yard. Moments later she came back there with me, "Lyric? What the fuck is wrong with you? Why you out there bussin and shit? Blowin' up the spot?" I slammed the door closed and walked over to the drawer and tossed her dildo on the bed. Moments later, I stripped down and bent over on the bed, "Fuck me," I said as I propped myself up and waited for her to put it in. She laughed, "Damn, Lyric," she said, "I see you horny as hell right now, huh?" I got up and pushed her down onto the bed, ripping her clothes off of her. After I had grabbed the toy, I rubbed it around her lips and then pushed it into her mouth slowly. She wrapped her lips around it and bobbed her head on it slowly, and I leaned over and joined her. We took turns placing our lips on it, kissing each other from time to time in the process.

I ran my hands down her chest until I got to her box and as she sucked on the dildo, I put my tongue inside of her until she started moaning. I licked all around it the way I loved to be touched. The way Nas and Junie did to me whenever they went down on me and made me cum in minutes. I looked up and caught a glimpse of her face as the toy was in her mouth and her eyes rolled back into her head. Just then, I got up and took the toy from her and put it inside of her and strapped it onto my waist. For a moment, I felt like Nas. The way he fucked me when I went to the prison. Hard, ruthless and without a care for how I felt. I pinned her legs behind her head, and as she screamed out, I put my hands around her throat, squeezing her neck tight and then releasing it. She collapsed her legs around my waist, and as soon as I felt them shake, I knew she was seconds away from her climax. Afterward, she snatched the strap on off me and worked me over. It was what I wanted and for whatever reason she didn't want to fuck me before, it was no longer there. If she had the same poison I had then there was no point in holding anything back anymore, and if she didn't give in, I would have taken it from her. She pulled my hair and slapped my ass, and I nearly yelled out Junie's name as she pushed my back down further so she could go in deeper. "Fuck me," I yelled out as she went in harder and pushed my face down into the pillow. I came moments later.

We lay together on the bed; her thick thighs stretched out over mine as our naked bodies glistened under the glow of the moon shining through the window. "I'm mad at myself that I waited this long for that to happen," she said, stroking my hair with her hands. "When are we getting money again?" I asked, stroking myself with my hand.

"This Friday. You ready, huh? You need money?"

"Nah, I'm good. I just don't give a fuck right now, you know? If we don't have to wait, then let's get it in. Fuck it."

"Aight. Now, what was up with that Deeko shit earlier?"

"That nigga was just getting' on my nerves. Every time I came over here, he was muggin' me like he had a problem, so I wanted to address it. I just got tired of it, you feel me?"

"I hear you."

"Besides, all those niggas are bitches, and if it came down to it, they probably wouldn't even fire they shit. Muthafuckas out here ain't hard; they just think they are because nobody tests them. That's all it is.

She didn't respond as we lay together in the bed. I could tell she was in deep thought about something, but I had my own thoughts to worry about. My mind wouldn't let me believe that anybody else but Nas gave me the virus and the fact that Prince may have it as well was enough to drive my desire to kill him more than anything else.

For the rest of the week, every time I came around the family they knew something was off. My interaction with Prince was limited to hugs and kisses with nothing else behind it. Stacey knew something was off, but after she realized I wasn't going to give her anything, she stopped trying. A part of me started to blame her for my sickness, but I knew that she had nothing to do with it. The only thing she did was urge me to go to the doctor, and the fact that I went had nothing to do with me contracting the virus. I had it either way, but I just didn't know how to come to terms with it. Dr. Carter left voicemails every day since I left her office, pleading with me to go to the HIV clinic and to get Prince tested. I wouldn't be able to handle it if he came down with the same poison I had, but I knew it was something I had to take care of.

Serena walked into the kitchen as I held the refrigerator door open. She cleared her throat to let me know she was in there with me. I looked at the door as she stood there with her arms across her chest, "What is wrong with you?" I pulled the milk out and sat down at the table with a bowl of cereal in front of me, "Nothing," I said, filling my bowl to the top with marshmallow oaties. She sat down next to me,

"What do you mean nothing?"

"The opposite of something."

She glared at me, "Don't be a smart-ass, Lyric." I took a bite of cereal as she waited for an explanation. "Well?"

"Well, what?"

"Damn it, Lyric! You've been walking around here barely talking to me. Barely saying anything to Mama and hardly even interacting with Prince. I mean, what it is? Are you tired of us being here? You want us gone?"

"Nah, it ain't nothing like that."

"I can't tell, Lyric. By the way you walking around here, it's hard to believe anything else."

"It's not that at all. I just got some stuff on my mind, that's all."

I coughed into my sleeve for a moment then continued eating.

"Bullshit, Lyric."

"What?"

"Bullshit! You expect us just to keep walking around here feeling like we are not wanted? I mean, nobody wants to live anywhere they aren't wanted so if you want us to leave just say it."

"I told you that is not what it is."

I continued eating my cereal as she impatiently sat in her seat, waiting for more of an explanation, but I had no intentions of telling her. This was something that I wanted to go away and since I knew it wasn't, I wanted to keep it as silent as possible. I wanted to handle it on my own. Suddenly, Serena jumped up from her seat, "Fuck it, Lyric. We will be out of your way." I knocked the box of cereal off the table. It flew against the wall as the contents inside the box fell to the ground and scattered across the floor. She spun around just in time to see tears form in my eyes, "I'm dying, aight? I'm fuckin' dyin! That's what it is!" I swung my hand, and the bowl full of cereal flew off the table and crashed to the floor. Serena looked at the mess I caused and then focused on me,

"What do you mean you're dying?"

"I have HIV, Serena. I got the fuckin' HIV virus."

She put her hand over her mouth and shook her head, her eyes bubbling with tears. She walked over to me slowly and put her arms around me. I cried, but I didn't reach back for her. This is another reason I didn't want to tell them. I knew they would feel sorry for me and in turn, make me feel sorrier for myself. "How long have you had it? I mean, how did you get it? Who?" I moved her away from me,

"Look, this is why I didn't want to tell you or Mama. I knew y'all would have questions that I just can't fuckin' answer right now."

"So, what? What are you going to do now? Does Prince have it?"

"Fuck. I don't know, Rena. I don't know. I gotta find out, but look, don't tell Mama shit, aight? Don't tell her because I'm not ready for the questions."

"Don't tell her? You know she feels the same way I did. Like you were getting tired of us."

"Well, just clear it up. Let her know that is not the case and make her believe it."

"Lyric?"

"Rena, I'm serious. Do not tell her, aight? Don't."

She sighed and wiped her eyes, "Okay. I won't tell her."

I reached down and cleaned up the mess I made with the cereal, and she leaned in to help me, "Listen, Lyric. Whatever you need and however I can help, just let me know, okay? You're my sister, and I know we aren't that close, but I just wanted you to know that you aren't going to go through this alone." I hugged her back, knowing all along that I would never use her for her help. I didn't even want her to know what I was going through, but I didn't want her to think I didn't want them around, so I had to tell her. I didn't want them going back home just to be an easy target for Nas.

Later that day, I took Prince to the HIV clinic. The women there gave me advice on protected sex and every other precaution I needed to take now that I was an HIV patient, but everything they told me went in one ear and out the other. Personally, I just wanted this shit to be over as quick as possible but in the meantime, I didn't care about anything else. They pricked my son and drew his blood, but oddly enough, he didn't even cry. I laughed when I thought about everything it took for Dr. Carter to draw my blood. With that, they told me they would have his results in a few weeks, but they wanted to meet with me again next week. I smiled and told them okay, knowing good and well that I wasn't coming back unless Prince's results were positive. I heard Big Mama as I drove home. She was scolding me for being hard-headed, but I turned the volume on the radio up. I wasn't in the mood to hear her right now. My mind was set directly on what I needed to do, and right now, Nas was the only person my mind could focus on. *Slow death?* I said to myself as Prince smacked one of his toys on the window. I glanced at him through the rearview, and he looked right back at me with a straight face. His innocence enraged me even more.

Chapter 11

"Lyric, you aight?"

"I'm good."

  I rode quietly in the car all the way to our spot. I mean, I didn't usually say much anyway, but this time I was more focused than before. I just wanted to get in and get all the money we could without wasting any time. I wasn't in the mood for the dancing and shit, especially if one of the girls wanted to fuck. It was only four of us this time, including Malley and I, so we all rode in the same car. We went to a small city just outside of Rockwall. One of the girls met two guys at a strip club and got them to come chill with us for a while.

"Lucy, how you know these niggas again?" Malley asked.

"Strip club. They were throwin' twenties and shit at some of them hoes on the stage, so I went over to them to see what was up. They walked me outside, and they both had a fucking Benz with some smooth ass chrome wheels and shit. From what I could tell, they had bread."

"Squares?"

"Nah, I mean, not like the last niggas. They seem like some regular ass muthafuckas. Nothing special."

  We arrived at a small motel that looked like shit on the outside. "What the fuck?" I asked as we pulled in. Two of the letters were out of light bulbs as we drove into the parking lot. "Malley, for real?" I asked. She looked at Lucy as Lucy responded, "I didn't know they were bringing us here." Malley stopped the car just beyond the entrance, "This shit looks like the place they take muthafuckas before they get killed." Grass grew in random spots of the parking lot and the red paint on the doors was chipped off, exposing the large wood that was just beneath it. "Hell no," Quandra said, "I'm not going in there. Fuck around and catch AIDS and shit just by breathing the air."

She didn't know my situation so I couldn't get mad at her, but I was ready to turn around and put the gun to her face. "Bitch, stop being funny," Lucy said as she laughed, "come on. These niggas got money and we trying to get paid, so let's just go in there and see what they are on." Malley parked the car, and we all got out and headed to the number. He opened the door; his locks flowed from his head in every direction with gold tips at the end of them. He smiled, "Whassup, ladies? Come on in." I walked in first as the rest of them came in after me. The other man inside looked just like the first one, except he was darker and his locks weren't golden at the tip. He had tattoos on his forearms as he sat in the chair right next to the bed. Lucy came in and spoke right with him,

"Why the fuck you got us in this bummy ass roach motel??"

"I'm married, and my wife got all those hotels in the city on lock. This was the only spot we could go to get this party goin', you know what I'm sayin?"

"Bummy. Ass. Motel."

He laughed, "Aye, you acting like we about to spend the fuckin' night here or something. We came here for a good time and shit, so chill with all that and show us why y'all came here."

Lucy stepped back next to Quandra, and they stripped down to their underwear. "Yeah," he said, "that's all I'm sayin. Bring yo' lil thick ass over here." Lucy walked over to him, and when Quandra sat on the other man's lap, I pulled my pistol out. "Look, I really don't have time for this shit today, aight? Y'all thought we were about to strip for y'all and shit but fuck that, y'all niggas strip." The two men looked at each other and then burst out laughing, "Bitch, are you crazy? You must be crazy. Now, put that fuckin' gun up before you scare these bitches in here." Malley looked at me out of the corner of her eye as Lucy and Quandra were confused momentarily. Suddenly, they stood up off the men's lap and backed towards us as Malley pulled her pistol out, "You heard her. This shit is not a game, STRIP!"

They didn't move until we both chambered a bullet in our guns and after that, they slowly began removing their shirts. They were both riddled with tattoos all over their chests and abs, and moments later, they dropped their pants. Their dicks hung low, and Lucy shook her head,

"Fuck, Lyric! Shit!"

"Bitch shut the fuck up. We came here to get money, not dick. You get that shit on yo' time or prostitute yo' ass out to Deeko's men."

"What?"

"You heard me."

"Ladies!" Malley yelled out, "this is not the time for that shit! Lucy, grab what's in their pants. Quandra, go check their car."

The two of them did as they were told as we stood there with our guns aimed directly at them. "Do y'all think y'all are going to get away with this? Really? Y'all must not know who y'all fuckin' with." I stepped closer to them, slowly, relishing the opportunity to fire my pistol and end his life, "I don't give a fuck who you are. What you should be worried about is who I am." The man was on his knees in front of me with his hands behind his head. He smiled and blew a kiss at me as I stepped closer to him.

"Lyric," Malley yelled out, "relax, baby. Relax."

"Yeah, baby, you heard what that bitch said. Relax."

Before I could react, Quandra walked back in with two bags in her hand, "Credit cards and cash, y'all. We good."

Lucy took the money they had inside their pockets and stuffed it in her bra, "We good here, too." Malley tossed the two girls some rope to tie them up to the bed. "Rope?" one of the men said as he started laughing, "Damn, y'all bitches are serious, huh? A got-damned rope, bruh. These bitches got a rope!" Lucy tied one of the men up, and as Quandra worked on the other one, I noticed something. The non-verbal communication they had going on between each other became completely evident. "What the fuck was that?" I asked, stepping closer to them.

"What was what?"

"Don't play stupid! I saw the motion you made to him with your eyes."

"What?"

"Oh, you think I'm stupid, right?"

"Lyric?" Malley asked curiously, "What's up, girl? You aight?"

I took my eyes off the man that Quandra was tying up, and suddenly, she was flung to the side of the room. When I glanced back at him, he dove under the bed and without thinking twice, I fired my pistol. The bullet seemed to leave the barrel in slow motion and pierced his chest. Lucy jumped as Quandra and Malley looked in horror as the man slouched over onto the ground and blood poured from his body. "Fuck!" Malley said out loud, "Grab the shit! Grab the shit and let's go!"

We rushed out of the motel room and got into the car; seconds later, we sped off. "Lyric! Lyric, what the hell!?" Lucy yelled from the back seat.

"He was making a move!"

"If you let us check the room in the beginning then we woulda caught that shit! Fuck! You have been on some shit all fuckin day!"

I spun around and pointed the pistol at her, "Yeah, I been on some shit and what the fuck are you gonna do it about it, huh?"

"Oh my God, Malley, you need to calm yo' bitch down. She got the wrong one."

"Oh, I do? I'll put one right through you just like I did that nigga back in the room, keep fuckin' with me."

"Lyric, yo, just chill," Quandra said, trying to diffuse the situation.

Malley chimed in, "Lyric, just relax, aight? All y'all, just chill the fuck out!"

I turned around in my seat as Malley sped down the highway. My hands were shaking as I began to realize what I'd just done. I had put everybody with me in danger and possibly ended somebody else's life. Silence flooded the car as Malley drove back to her apartment. Lucy tossed her the money she took from the guys and got out of the car without speaking to anyone. Moments later, she got in her car and left. Quandra followed right behind her and left me in the car with Malley. "Lyric, you wanna tell me what the fuck all that was about?" I shook my head as the street illuminated both of us inside the car. Suddenly, it was just time.

"His name is Nas, right?"

"What?"

"Nas. The nigga you used to fuck with back in Ohio."

Her mouth hung open. "Wait, I'm trying to understand what is going on right now."

"The nigga you used to fuck with in Ohio, the one that moved to Milwaukee. His name is Nas. Nasir Jones."

"You know him?"

"Know him? I was with him for about a year."

I thought she would be a little upset when she found out my past with him, but she didn't even seem fazed by it. I let her know that the little boy she saw at my house was actually his son.

"What? That's his son!? You know what, I knew he favored Nas, and I said it to myself, I just didn't think it was his. It was too big of a coincidence for me."

We ended up chilling in the car for at least an hour, talking and understanding each other. We eventually got to the point that I had to tell her about the infection. I wanted to let her know why I was so erratic and out of character, and she understood.

"I did the same thing. I've had it for about five years now, and it's in the dormant stage, so who the fuck knows what's going to happen next."

She helped me understand what she went through when she found out, and in turn, she knew where I was coming from. It felt good to have somebody who knew exactly what I was going through, but in the process I found out that we actually had the same intentions. She had ill will towards Nas just as much as I did, and we were both plotting ways to make him pay for poisoning us, but when I told her my plans, she was all for it. She wanted to kill him for revenge; I just wanted Prince to remain safe, especially if his test came back negative.

"Shit, I'm down for whatever, Lyric. Just let me know and I'm there."

Chapter 12

She straightened shit out with Quandra and Lucy, but we all had to lay low for a while because of how I fucked up. It had been about a week since our last heist and for the time being, there wasn't any extra attention coming our way from the police or anyone else. I got a phone call from the clinic later that day,

"Hello Miss Sutton, this is Amy Price. Your son's results came back, and he tested negative for the virus. Now, I'm not sure how to explain that because it almost never happens, but your son is completely healthy. Now, as far as you go, if you would like to come back in this Saturday, we can get you set up with an official counselor."

"Ok, I'll come this Saturday."

"How is 2 pm?"

"2 pm is fine."

"Ok, we got you down for 2 pm. See you then."

I had no intention at all of going to the clinic. My son had a clean bill of health and to me, that is all that mattered. My next thing to do was to work on taking care of Nas. I called Vinny, but his phone went straight to voicemail. This was the third time I had called him in the past few days, but I hadn't heard back from him, and it was definitely out of his character. I was uneasy when I called him later that night and got the same result. The only way to put my mind at ease was to head to Milwaukee myself just to check things out.

Early the next morning, I headed back to the city. It had been almost six months since I'd been back and I was anxious to see it again with my own eyes. Things looked just the way they did when I left. Big Mama's house was still kept up. The grass was cut and the bushes were trimmed, it even looked as if the outside had a fresh paint job on it. *That nigga Vinny has been earning his keep*, I said to myself as I pulled into the driveway. His car wasn't around, so I figured he had to be at work. I walked in, and the living room was spotless. I smiled, imagining that Big Mama herself had come to clean it up. That is just how good it looked. I walked into the kitchen as nostalgic feelings flooded through my mind. Flashbacks of Big Mama in the kitchen, cooking over the stove brought a smile to my face.

"Lyric, take your elbows off that table! You know I raised you better than that!"

I laughed when I remembered how she used to swing the belt at me just to scare me. I made my way into her room, and it still looked the same. The peace that always rested in the atmosphere whenever I walked in was still there as if it waited for me to come back. I walked over to the picture of Mama that was pinned between the dresser mirror and the frame. I picked it up and placed it in my pocket, "You won't mind if I take this, will you, Big Mama?" The peace agreed with my choice as I reached for my phone to dial Vinny's number again. It still went straight to voicemail, so I decided to leave and check out a few more places.

When I got outside, Shaunie was just headed up the cement steps on her way to the house. "Oh my God, Lyric?" She walked up to me and hugged me around the neck,

"It feels like I haven't seen you in forever."

I smiled, "Yeah, it's been a minute. You been aight?"

"Yeah, I been straight, I was just coming over to holler at Vinny because he wasn't answering his phone."

"I thought he was at work?"

"He must be, but I thought he had the day off."

"He ain't in there. You know he usually in the front playing his game and shit."

"Yeah, I know. But how is Rockwall?"

"Boring as hell."

We sat down on the porch,

"You had to know it was going to be like that, though."

"Yeah, but damn, you know? I'm about to fuckin' go crazy."

"Shit, at least it's safer than here. You know yo' boy Nas got out and that nigga been on a fuckin' rampage and shit."

"Yeah, I heard he got out. What he been doin?"

"He shut down the whole east side with this shit. Don't nobody go over there no more unless people is buyin'."

"Nobody new poppin' up?"

"Not really. It was a young cat that came out here trying to do something but after a while nobody saw him anymore. He either left or Nas took care of him."

"Damn. You know where he is at?"

"Who, Nas?"

"Yeah."

"Shit, same spot down off Buffum. Motherfuckas know where he at and shit but still don't test him."

"Aight. Well, I'm about to roll down to Vinny's job and holla at him."

"Ok, Lyric. It was good seeing you and when you see Vinny, tell that nigga I need my money!"

I laughed, "Aight."

We hugged each other, and I watched her walk down the block until she disappeared around the corner. Right after that, I called Vinny's phone again, but it went straight to voicemail for the third time. "Fuck, Vinny," I said out loud as I got in the car and drove off. When I got to his job, they told me that Vinny hadn't shown up today. "Uh, Vinny was scheduled to come in, but we haven't heard from him. If you do happen to see him, though, please tell him to call in. We don't want to have to let him go, but we will."

I left his job, and the nervousness crept into my heart as I headed back to Big Mama's house. I hoped that his car was parked outside in the driveway when I got there, but to my dismay, his spot was still empty. I glanced around the neighborhood before I got out and headed back to the front door. The house was just the way I left it, and suddenly, a sickening feeling pumped through my stomach. *His room*, I thought to myself, *I didn't even go in there when I got here the first time.* I crept down the hallway to his door and put my ear to it, listening for any movement inside. When I didn't hear any, I twisted the knob on the door. The covers were thrown off his bed, and his dresser was turned over to its side. When I walked in, I saw him with his back against the wall and his head slouched down to his chest.

"Vinny!"

I yelled his name out and rushed to him as blood just began to dry on the side of his mouth, "Vinny! Oh my God, Vinny!" He slowly lifted his head up and his eyes opened just a little bit. I searched his body for the wound; a knife was stuck in his side just below his armpit. Blood soaked his shirt, and as his eyes opened wider, he struggled to breathe even more.

"Hold on, Vinny! Just hold on, aight!"

I fumbled my phone as I pulled it out of my pocket to call the police. "Vinny, hang on, aight! They are coming!" His breathing became harder and harder as I saw the panic in his eyes while he coughed out more blood. "They are coming! It's going to be alright, Vinny! It's going to be alright!" Moments later, I heard sirens coming closer to the house and before I knew it, the paramedics were inside, pulling me away from him. I leaned against the wall as they worked to keep him alive and his blood spilled out onto the floor. Just then, they lifted him onto the stretcher and rushed him out of the house. I trailed them all the way to the hospital as tears blurred my vision and almost caused me to crash multiple times.

We all arrived, and they rushed him to emergency as I stood in the waiting room, pacing back and forth nervously. *This can't be happening*, I said to myself, *this can't be happening!* I waited there for a few hours until the doctor came out of the room solemnly. I shook my head in disbelief before he could even get the words out, "No, no, noooo!" I yelled out as the doctor tried to calm me down. "I'm sorry, I'm so sorry," he said, attempting to settle me but it wasn't enough. Vinny's dried blood was on my hands and that, in itself, said everything that needed to be said about the way he died.

Chapter 13

The ride back to Rockwall was the longest ride of my life. My phone had been ringing off the hook ever since the word about Vinny's death started circulating, but I kept forwarding the calls. I wasn't in a mood to talk and right now, all I wanted to do was murder Nas. I wanted him off the earth because he was terrorizing everyone in the city that knew me just so they would tell him where I was at. I knew that was the reason, and I knew they killed him because he wouldn't tell them my location. That alone drove a knife through my own heart, and it was yet another family member that I would end up blaming myself for their death.

I pulled up to my apartment at around 1 am. The light in the front room was still on, and I knew either Stacey or Serena was still up, waiting for me to return. I took a deep breath and walked in, and Stacey stood to her feet with tears in her eyes, "I'm so sorry, Lyric. I'm so sorry." She rushed to me and hugged me as I put my arms around her, but at that moment I was numb to everything. I was numb to her tears, my feelings, and everything else that was going on around me.

The next day, I made funeral arrangements for Vinny and asked Shaunie to be the point for me. I paid for everything myself, but I knew that going back to his funeral would be the wrong thing to do. I figured that Nas would expect me to be there and use that like cheese to draw me out, but my whole thing was always about being one step ahead of the enemy at all times. It killed me that I wasn't able to be there, but I knew it was for the best and I know that Vinny would understand that, too. It was hard for me to accept that two of the closest people to me had died in the past few years, and just when I was beginning to cope with Big Mama's death, Vinny turns up dead right with her. I called Malley and let her know what happened, and right then she was ready to make a move on Nas. She figured this was the best time to do it, but she knew we had to have a good plan before we charged in; that is what I was best at. We decided to do one more heist to get a little more bread before we took off to do our own thing in Milwaukee.

Later that day, I showed up to Malley's spot. Deeko and his boys weren't around when I got out the car, so I figured they weren't fucking with us anymore because of me, but I couldn't care less. Upstairs, Quandra and Lucy sat in the living room and a cloud of marijuana smoke swarm over me as soon I stepped inside. I closed the door behind me and waited to see what they would do. After a few tense moments, Quandra finally smiled, "We good, Lyric," she said. Lucy got up and shook my hand, "We good, fam. Malley cleared all that shit up. Those periods fuck everything up, trust me, I know. I am ready to break a bitch face whenever that shit come." They all laughed it off, and I walked to the back where Malley was chilling.

"A period? Really?"

She laughed, "If it's one thing hoes understand, it's when that period come on us. Mood swings like a muthafucka."

"Yeah, so whassup? We got some marks?"

"Yeah, we got a couple on standby. You sure you ready for it?"

"Yeah, I'm ready. I got that outburst shit under control now."

She smiled and leaned in to kiss me on my lips, "Aight, cool. Well, we just gon' chill for a minute until we get word that everything is straight, then we will head out."

"Aight."

We passed the time fucking and smoking until Lucy came back into the room with the news, "Aye, they ready for us. The chick wants us to meet them downtown at the Q."

With that, we got up and got ourselves ready to meet them downtown. The Q was a mid-range hotel in Rockwall that usually teens went to when they wanted to fuck and didn't have anywhere else to go. The hotel managers pretty much let anything slide as long as you didn't mind paying them a little extra. We walked outside to the car, and I glanced over at Deeko's normal spot again.

"The fuck them niggas at? They quit?"

She laughed, "After that shit you pulled with them a little while ago, they vamped. You scared them off and shit."

"Soft ass niggas."

"Shit, it's about time to move around from here anyway. We hit enough licks for now, so we need to go before it starts getting too hot."

It was 10 pm when we drove into the parking lot of the Q. It was usually pretty packed on a Saturday night, but this time it was oddly much thinner than normal. We all got out the truck Malley had just gotten. She switched the car out after I popped the dude at the last heist just in case there were any cameras around. Alisha waved to us when they saw us from the front door, and we followed her in. "These niggas good?" Malley asked as we walked in. "Yeah, they got bread," she responded without looking at her. I squinted my eyes at her as she walked a few feet in front of us and opened the door. Inside, a group of niggas stood around waiting for us to come in. On first glance, they were clean cut dudes that seemed out of place, but as they spoke I realized this wasn't their first time doing something like this.

The girls went through their regular routine, undressing and stripping for the men while they searched them for weapons. Malley and I looked around the room to make sure there was nothing they had hidden anywhere, and once everything was clean, we stood back and let them work. One of the men spoke to me, "What, y'all ain't coming over here?

What's up with that? Y'all too good for us?" I smiled, and moments later, I felt a pistol to the back of my head.

"Who's soft now, bitch?"

By the voice, I knew who it was. Deeko stood behind me with a chrome desert eagle pressed to the back of my skull. Another dude grabbed Malley and took the gun off her before they threw her against the wall. Quandra and Lucy stood up, half naked, with their mouths hung open as Alisha smiled and walked to the side next to Deeko. I knew something was up with her as soon as she waved us in. She played us from the start. I shot daggers at her and then glanced at Deeko. "Oh, don't stop the party now," he said, "Y'all bitches get back on my niggas and fuck with them. Y'all here so y'all might as well do what the fuck you came for." They didn't move, and Deeko raised his voice, "Did y'all hear me? I'm not fucking playin'; y'all hoes get back on my niggas." Quandra and Lucy straddled the men in front of them as Deeko slid the pistol off my waist, "Now, you won't be needing this, will you?" he said as he laughed and spun me around.

"So, I'm soft, huh? I'm a bitch ass nigga, right? I mean, that's what you said, ain't it? You said, 'Deeko, you're a bitch ass nigga.' Am I wrong?" I remained silent, and he leaned in closer to me,

"Bitch. Am. I. Wrong."

"Nope, you're not wrong. You are every bit of a bitch ass nigga."

He laughed, "Yes! I love it! Even with a gun to her fucking head, she still got the nerve to talk shit. Well, guess what," he said, rubbing my ass with his hand, "I wanted to fuck you from day one. Remember that? When I tried to holla at you and you dissed me? Well, guess what? Deeko gets what he wants but this time, we got an audience." Malley yelled out, "Deeko, leave her alone." He pointed the gun at her, "Did I tell you to talk? Because if I did, I'm telling you right now to shut the fuck up." He looked at Quandra and Lucy as they watched us, "The fuck y'all looking at? Grind on my niggas! Damn!" They spun around and continued dancing as Malley looked on in complete horror. We had gotten away with this for a while, and there was no telling how long they had been doing this, but I guess all things must come to an end. Deeko turned to look at Malley, "See, I'm not going to touch you, Malley, even though you are fine as a muthafucka. But since you tried to check me in front of this bitch, you're still getting raped, it's just that we are getting you in another way. My niggas are cleaning out yo' apartment right now," he said laughing, "so um, yeah, all them weapons and shit? All that money? That'll be coming with us."

He turned back towards me. "Now you," he said as he handed his gun to Alisha and pulled his pants down, "turn around." I smiled and spun around and bent over for him. "Oh," he said, "you want it too, huh? Aight." Just then, he stuck his dick deep inside of me, and I smiled, winking at Malley. I didn't want it, but he didn't know that with each pump, he was filling himself with the HIV virus. He smacked my ass, and I pushed myself against, even more, making sure he felt every inch of my pussy. *A slow death*, I said to myself as he fucked me from behind while everybody watched. I looked over at Alisha as she smirked at me, seemingly enjoying every second of what I was going through. None of it bothered me at all though because I knew that the moment he found out, he was going to regret the day he fucked me. And Alisha? I could tell those two were fucking so it was just a matter of time before she got what she deserved, too. He pulled out and came on my back and moments after he was done, they all left the room.

"Shit! That fuckin' bitch!" Quandra yelled out, "Wait until I see her ass again! I'm fucking her up!"

I couldn't help but laugh to myself at the irony of what just happened. A few years ago, Quandra was the one setting me up, and now karma found its way back to her. It was just fucked up that I had to be here when it did. Malley rushed over to me, "You aight?" I smiled, "I'm good, you already know."

She shook her head and seconds later we got dressed and left. That was the last time we were going to pull a heist in Rockwall.

Chapter 14

Her apartment was in shambles. Dressers were turned over; her mattress was ripped down the middle and on the sides. There were holes kicked in the walls inside her closet and everything was scattered all over the floor. "Weak ass niggas," she murmured as she went to all the spots she kept her money hidden. She pulled back a handful of hundred dollar bills that were rolled up inside of a sock and taped beneath the dresser. "Fuckin idiots didn't even search the whole spot," she said, tucking the money into her pocket.

We walked outside in the middle of the day, scanning the area for any sign of Deeko. I knew he wouldn't be around, though. He talked big shit back at the hotel, but the likelihood of him showing back up over here was highly unlikely. She glared in the direction of his apartment, her red hair fluttering in the wind. I could tell what she was thinking, and she had a right to want to go over there and kill every last one of them. Just then, she headed in that direction, but I pulled her arm, "Malley, nah. We can't fuck with them right now. They got all yo' pistols and mine, too. Just chill, we'll get them later, aight." It took her a few moments before she took her eyes off of his apartment and eventually I got her to leave.

"I think we need to chill on the heists and shit for a minute, Malley. What you think?"

"My words exactly. Shit is gettin' a little out of hand right now, so I feel you. That bitch Alisha though? Damn. All these niggas are gettin' theirs, I swear to God, Lyric. On everything, I'm coming back on their ass, hard."

"Yo, that's cool and all, but honestly, I think we need to start focusing on Nas. They will get what's coming to them, but right now, you know what I'm sayin, since we on a break from that shit, we might as well see what we can do with him."

She looked at me as we stopped at a red light,

"Aight, yeah, we can do that. He's in Milwaukee, right?"

"Yeah. I know exactly where he is."

"Word. Aight then, yeah, let's move on that nigga."

We rode back to my apartment, and when I got in, nobody else was home. Serena was usually at work during this time of day and Stacey had taken Prince with her to the store. We sat down on the couch, and she flipped on the television with the remote. "So," she said, "what you got planned?" I looked to the right, replaying a number of different scenarios in my head involving what we could do. I figured we would need another person to help pull everything off since Nas knew both of us. I thought back to the way he used me to draw Big Tuck in but that alone took months to set up, and we didn't have that kind of time. Besides, I'm pretty sure he would know something was up if we took the same approach to lure him in.

I reached for my phone and scanned through the list of contacts as Malley patiently flipped through the channels. My eyes glued on his name when I scrolled to it. *Loc*, I said to myself. That nigga wasn't dumb, though, but I knew he had a soft spot for me. I had come across him plenty of times, and he could've killed me at any moment, but he didn't. Maybe I can use him and Man-Man? I looked at Malley and said,

"I got an idea."

"I'm listening."

"Since I know that Nas wants Prince, I say we use that to our advantage. We use Prince to lure those niggas out, and when they get to us, then that's that."

"Hold up," she said, turning towards me, "use Prince as bait? Are you serious right now? Is the virus fuckin' with your head again?"

"Nah, I got this. I mean, look, the only thing that will get Nas's attention is me, Prince, or his money, and honestly, I don't even know how to get to his bread anymore. He moves his stash houses so much, and if we hit the wrong one, then we're done."

"Lyric, I'm sayin', though, Prince? That's your son."

"I know who he is; just trust me on this, aight? Just trust me."

I could tell she was uneasy but what else could she say? He was my son, and she didn't have the authority to come in and say anything different. I watched her squirm in her seat a little bit as she mindlessly flipped through channels before fessing up, "Girl, I'm just fuckin' with you. There ain't no way in the world I was going to take Prince back to Milwaukee." She laughed,

"I knew you were full of shit. I was just going to chill and wait until you realized what you were sayin'."

"But the thing about it is we have to make him believe that Prince is there, which means I'ma have to go there and show my face for a minute, so he thinks we are both back."

"Aight, so what? Am I coming with you?"

"Hell, yeah. We both going back to the city together."

"Bet. It's going down."

She had a wide grin on her face as she scooted closer to me and kissed me on the neck. "Nah, we can't do that right here. I don't know when Prince and Stacey will show up." She sighed, "Aight." Just then, I grabbed her by the hand and led her into my room. One of the things she took from her apartment was her toy and at that moment, I was happy that she did. It wasn't real dick, but I had learned to settle for it since it was pretty much the only dick I would be able to have.

I didn't go to any of the sessions, so I wasn't exactly sure what I could and couldn't do, sexually. They had called my phone almost every day since I got Prince's results, but I couldn't care less about it. If I was going to die, I was going to die, and there was no point in prolonging it at all.

Malley laid in the bed when we were finished, and I walked out into the front room. Stacey and Prince still hadn't come back from the store yet, so I walked around in my bra and panties. I stood in front of a mirror, admiring my thickness but realizing that it may not always be there, especially if the virus turned into AIDS. I sighed and almost came to tears until I heard Big Mama's voice, "Girl, go and put some clothes on with yo' nasty behind!" I laughed when she fussed at me, but I was surprised that was all she said. I waited around to hear more but silence rang throughout the house until keys rattled at the door. Before they could get into the apartment, I walked back to my bedroom and closed the door. "Malley, wake up. They're back."

Chapter 15

I let Stacey know that I was going back to Milwaukee for a couple of weeks. She was completely against the idea, but I told her that I needed to go back and take care of some things regarding Vinny's funeral and Big Mama's house. Eventually, she understood that it was something I had to do, and she would keep Prince under her watch until I came back. I picked him up in my arms,

"Hey, Mama's baby. I'm going away for a little while, alright? You be good and don't give G-Ma a hard time, okay?"

"Girl, please. Between him and you, I'd say that you were the one that gives me the hardest time."

I laughed and kissed her on the cheek before I left. It wasn't a response that Big Mama would have given, but it was close enough. The ride back to Milwaukee was peaceful for the most part. Malley asked questions about shit almost the whole way there. For a moment, it seemed like she just wanted to come to the city to party a little bit, but I knew she would get refocused when the time came. Besides, we had a week or two to kill anyway so taking her out may not have been a bad thing at all. Nas would have been sure to know I was back in Milwaukee that way. When we got to Big Mama's house, I saw that the grass had grown into an unseemly sight. Inside the home, Vinny's room was still a mess, and the front room was still disorganized from the time the paramedics rushed in. After Vinny had died, I didn't do much here at all except lock up the house. I couldn't stand being there for much longer than I had to, knowing that three of the four people who lived in this house had all died within the last two years.

I stood in the living room, reminiscing on all the times I shared with them while we all lived here. The first time I snapped on Uncle Stew when he came home to check on Big Mama. I threatened him, saying if he was still strung out and any of Big Mama's stuff ended up missing that I was going to beat the shit out of him. He laughed and told me not to worry, and he was right. If it wasn't for my dumb ass mistake, maybe he would still be here right now. I saw Vinny on the couch playing video games, getting pissed off whenever he lost to the computer, "Man, Lyric, I can't stand this bullshit! This muthafuckin' game is cheating like a bitch, on everything! Fuckin' bullshit!" I laughed at how angry he would get while playing his games. Junie was the same way, though. Maybe it was just a guy thing because he was known to shatter his video game controllers into walls whenever things weren't going his way. Malley nudged me on my shoulder,

"This is a nice ass house, Lyric. Damn. Maybe we should just live here and shit."

"Nah. This ain't that type of house. We just here for right now."

She walked over and sat down on the couch in the same spot I imagined Vinny was seated and with that, I went into his room. The stench of dried blood hit my nose as soon as I walked down the hallway. I was apprehensive about going inside because of the last image that was in my mind when I walked in before, but I forced myself in. His bloodstain was against the wall and on the floor in the same spot I found him in when I finally checked his room. My imagination filled the room with chaos just as it was the day that he was rushed out of here on a stretcher. I wiped tears from my eyes and backed out of the room, not knowing how much more of the emotion I could take. It was hard to understand that there could be so much peace in one room of the house, but just down the hall, utter chaos. I let Malley know I was going to Big Mama's room to chill for a minute and in moments, I was fast asleep.

She stood just outside the door later that night, "Lyric, yo, I'm fuckin" starving. Let's get something to eat." I woke up and glanced at the time. It was almost 7 pm when I drug myself out of Big Mama's bed and walked down the hallway. I looked into Vinny's room but this time I wasn't as anxious as I was when I first came in. Maybe spending some time in Big Mama's room calmed me down a little bit. Afterward, I headed out to the front room with Malley and just a little while later we left. We drove down the neighborhoods as she glanced out the window like a tourist. "This shit kinda look like Akron," she said as we drove past the beat down houses in the city. It didn't take long for us to make it to Speed Queen. Speed Queen was a barbecue joint on the east side of Milwaukee, and they served some of the best ribs in the world, at least that's what I thought. When we got out the car, a couple people recognized me. "Suzy? Damn, where you been?" one of the girls said as she was heading to her car.

"Just out, doin' my thang."

"You still rappin?"

"Nah, not really."

"That's fucked up. You had some classics out here. I still remember when you came back and took over Remy's show. That shit was hard!"

I laughed at the thought, "Word. I appreciate you."

"Aight. Well, I'll holla at you."

Malley watched her as she drove off and then turned towards me, "You used to rap, too?" I looked off to the right, "Yeah. I mean, it was a while ago, though, you know? I haven't' really done anything since so I don't mention it." With that, we headed to the front line and that's when images of Block flooded through my mind. He was a security guard I knew from back in the day. He was the one that helped me get on stage and fuck up Remy's show when I came back from Chicago. *Maybe he could help,* I thought to myself as we stood in line. He could have had connections that went deeper than mine and if not that, I know that he wouldn't have a problem keeping us safe if need be. I just had to find out how to get in touch with him.

The sun began to set below the horizon as we sunk our teeth into the plate of ribs. "Damn, Lyric, you weren't lying. This shit is good." I wiped my mouth with a napkin and responded to her, "I told you. You know I wouldn't lead you wrong." As we ate, I thought about stopping by Onyx to see if Block was still working there. It was a long shot because most security guards don't stick around for that long, but if he wasn't there I was sure one of them could point us in the right direction. After we finished eating, we went to the club. I drove to the back the way I normally did whenever I showed up. I didn't see any sign of Block once we got there, but I got out and walked to the back door as Malley walked right beside me. The man at the door stood in front of us, preventing us from going any further.

"Can I help y'all?"

I spoke up, "I'm looking for Block."

"Who?"

"Block. A big ass nigga that works security here."

"Ain't nobody named Block that works here."

"Oh?" I said, looking just beyond him, "What y'all got goin' on in there tonight?"

"First of all, who are you and why are you asking so many questions?"

He stepped closer to us, but I pulled Malley back, "My bad, my nigga. I didn't mean anything by it; I was just seeing what was going on." He seemed to snarl at us as the streetlights began flickering on in the alley, "Well, walk to the fucking front and find out. This back here don't concern you." I tapped Malley on the side and then we walked back to the car. "Muthafucka's rude as a bitch up here," she said, peering back at the security guard. "Something is up with him," I said, "I could tell. Most niggas don't act like that at the back, even if you don't belong there." I started the engine, and suddenly, gunshots rang out. We ducked down in our seats just as more bullets rang out. I couldn't tell what direction they were coming from, but as soon as I heard a break in the shooting, I lifted my head up. The guard that was at the door was just gunned down as he laid right in the spot we were just standing. When I looked ahead, I saw two men in black hoodies pointing the gun at our car. I put my head down and went in reverse as fast as I could down the alley. As soon as we got to the street, I put it into drive and peeled off down the street. It was too dark to be able to see what was going on or who was shooting, but chances are, it was somebody that didn't give a fuck about who we were, but it didn't seem that any of it mattered. I just thanked God that we had gotten out of the way of their real target, but who knows, maybe I was the target, and he had just gotten in the way. In either case, I knew that walking around Milwaukee was no longer an option. If we were going to do anything, it had to be completely covert.

"So, it's clear that we are going to need some guns and shit, Lyric, especially if niggas are clappin' at us like that on a regular," she said as she slowly lifted her head up. The windshield had a few bullet holes at the top of it but nothing too major. She was right, though, we needed weapons if we were going to be here in the city. Nas probably had everyone on alert for me if I was ever to show up again. When we got back to the house, I called Shaunie, "Hey girl, it's me. Call me when you can." I knew she would probably know more about the city than I would since I had been gone for almost a year. Malley sat down in the front room as I went to the hall to get some supplies to clean Vinny's room. It was hard, almost like washing away memories, but I did the best job I could. Big Mama always kept ammonia around when she had to do deep cleaning, so I got to work. It took me about an hour to get everything as clean as I could.

Malley came into the room moments later. "You aight?" she asked just before I wiped a tear from my eye. "Yeah, I'm good. I'm good," I said to her. She took a deep breath, "We're going to get that nigga, Lyric. I promise you." I took the stuff back out of Vinny's room just as my phone rang. It was Shaunie.

"Whassup, Lyric."

"Hey, Shaunie. How are you doing?"

"About as good as I can be right now, you know? It's just not the same without him around."

"I feel you on that. It's going to take a while to get over it, I understand. He is going to be missed, without a doubt."

"Yeah," she paused for a moment, "but what's up? I know you didn't just call because you were bored."

"Nah, I didn't. I need to get in touch with Block. You remember him?"

"Block? Nah, not really."

"The big ass security guard I tried to hook you up with when I got back from Chicago."

"Oh, that nigga?" she laughed, "yeah, I remember him. Matter of fact, I still got his number and shit."

"You do? Man, I need to get that from you. I gotta holla at him real quick."

"Ok, but he doesn't live in the city no more."

"Damn, he doesn't?"

"Nah. He moved to Atlanta a little over a year ago now, but I can still give you his number."

"Aight."

"I'ma text it to you."

"Okay, that's cool."

"Aight."

"Aye, Shaunie. Be safe, aight?"

"Shit, you don't have to tell me that. I'm moving out of town next week. I've had enough of all this killing and shit. Milwaukee ain't gettin' no better no time soon."

"Movin'? Well, look, I'ma talk to you about that later, aight? Make sure you text me his number, though."

"Okay. I'm about to do it right now."

      The text came through as soon as we hung up and I called him, but it went straight to voicemail. "Yo, Block. It's yo' girl, Lyric. I need to talk to you, fam, so whenever you get this, please call me back, aight?" From that point, all I could do was sit and wait for him to return my call. I knew that there was really no way that I could get any weapons in the city by myself. I was sure that Nas had everything under tight surveillance, so my next best bet was Block. He was the guy I turned to whenever I got in a jam earlier in my life. He was actually the one who sold me the gun I used on the night Junie was killed. I walked over to the window, patiently waiting for him to call me back. Out the corner of my eye, I saw a car driving slowly up the street. I told Malley to shut the TV off so that there wouldn't be any lights on inside. The car crept slowly, and when it got in front of Big Mama's house, it stopped. It was an all-white Impala with heavily tinted windows. We both peered outside through a tiny opening on both sides of the curtain. The car stayed there for a few minutes and all of a sudden, the side door opened, and Man-Man got out of the car. He looked up and down the street and then glared at the house once again.

      After that, he headed towards the front door as my heart skipped a beat inside my chest. "Shhh," I said, glancing at Malley as we removed ourselves from the window. I heard his footsteps walk up the porch and then towards the front room window. His shadow was just in front of where we stood as he cupped his hand over the glass and leaned in. If I had a gun, I would have put it right in the window and shot him right in his forehead. Suddenly, the car horn blew, and he turned to walk away. We snuck back to our original spots near the window and watched him get in the passenger's seat as they drove off. "That was Man-Man," Malley said as she caught her breath.

"You know him?"

"Hell yeah. He's one of Nas's homies from Ohio. That nigga is a fuckin' terror, himself."

We sat back down on the couch, both too nervous to turn on the television or anything else until we felt it was safe. Just then, my phone rang, and it scared the shit out of both of us. I quickly reached for it on the couch,

"Hello?"

"Lyric? What's good, Ma?"

"Shit, Block. I'm chillin'."

"Chillin', huh? Last I heard, you were runnin' the city with Nas and shit."

"Well, a lot has changed since then, Block. A whole lot."

"Word?"

"Yeah, it's a long story, though, you know what I'm sayin'? I'll fill you in later, but I need to holla at you about something."

"Well, what's up?"

"I need some weapons, Block. Like, some pistols and shit. Automatics if you got them."

"You know I ain't in the Mil no more, right?"

"Yeah, but I figured you still had some connections here for that shit."

He sighed, "I mean, I do but—"

"Block, this shit has to be legit, like... I don't want Nas to know shit about it."

"Trust me, I know, and the person I'm thinking of don't even fuck with Nas. He on the south side."

"Aight."

"But the only thing is, you remember that house you found Prince in?"

"Yeah."

"Well, the nigga that you need to holla at is connected to them SA's."

"Fuck!"

It was like every hope that I had of getting my hands on something to help protect us was shattered right in front of me. I didn't know how I was going to get my hands on anything, knowing that those SA's would immediately remember me as soon as I stepped foot over there. "I know, Lyric. You're not going to want to go over there now, I mean, I know it happened a while ago but you still too hot to show yo' face." I sighed, "I know, man. I know." I looked over at Malley as she scrolled through her phone and that's when I got the idea,

"Say, Block, if I can send somebody else over there, you think it would be a problem?"

"Somebody like who?"

"Somebody I can trust."

"Nah, I don't see a problem with it. Just let me know who and I'll take it from there."

"Aight. Yo, stay by your phone, I'ma hit you right back."

I spoke with Malley and told her the situation so she could understand why I couldn't go over there and get the weapons myself. She understood, and she didn't have a problem with it at all. The only issue was getting her over there, and that's when she brought up Quandra. "Shit, if it's not you, I trust Quandra. She lived here, and she knows her way around. Besides that, I've known her the longest. I trust her." I thought about Chicago for a moment but quickly removed it from my mind. That was the past, and she told me she was different, and during the time we were finessing niggas in Rockwall, she never showed any signs of transgressing. "Aight, let's see if Quandra will take you out there then."

She called Quandra, and we explained the situation to her. She had moved from Rockwall to Waukegan since we both left to go to Milwaukee, but she was all for it. "That's it? Yeah, I'll come through for you. I fucking missed y'all bitches anyway," she said when we put her on speaker phone. With that, I called Block again and let him know the situation. He told me to give him until tomorrow, and he would call back with all the information we needed to meet the SA and pick up the stuff. Time was running out for us, and I knew Nas had an idea that I was back in town. It was all I needed, just for him to believe that I was so I could use it to my advantage. I still didn't know if the shooting outside of Onyx had anything to do with me or not, but if I had to guess, I would say that it did. The guard was just in the wrong place at the wrong time, but I was going to be ready if any of that shit happened again. Suddenly, I began coughing, and my stomach felt queasy, so I laid down on the couch. "Lyric, are you gon' be alright?" Malley asked when she glanced at me. The moonlight from above us shined down on me through a crack in the curtains. I felt like it was Big Mama trying to get my attention.

"Yeah, I'ma be straight. Yo, just keep a lookout, aight? I don't know if those niggas will make another run through here or not."

"Aight," she said, leaning back on the couch as she rubbed my thighs.

One way or the other, I knew I was going to see Big Mama again soon. I started to think about the God that she always thanked and prayed to when she was here, and as the thought of death began to loom larger in my mind, I knew that I was going to find out the truth about him. I became nervous just at the thought as sorrow crept through my body. I turned my head to get the moonlight off of my face, ignoring the glow as I had done for the majority of my life. Even then, the tugging on my heart increased even more, and I couldn't tell if it was Big Mama or God himself, but either way, I felt it stronger than I had before. I coughed once more but this time it was more viscous than before. "You need some water?" Malley said as she sat up on the couch. I shook my head no and repositioned myself on the couch, away from the glow. I had to do what I came here for. This wasn't for me anymore; this was for Prince's safety, and I felt that no God would be able to keep him safe if Nas was still around.

Chapter 16

Quandra came by later the next day. We told her to let us know when she was on her way so we could keep a look out for anything suspicious going on around the neighborhood. "What up, Lyric? What up, Malley? I missed y'all bitches!" she said when she came in the house with a big ass smile on her face. She hugged both of us before she sat down on the couch. "Where Big Mama at, Lyric?" She didn't know that she had passed away almost two years ago, and I didn't expect her to know. We weren't close at all, especially since she crossed me in Chicago.

"She died almost two years ago. Cancer."

She put her hand over her mouth, "Are you serious? I'm so sorry, Lyric. I didn't even know." I glanced at the window, then looked back at her.

"It's cool; you didn't know. She in a better place and she's not feeling pain anymore, so I'm good. You ready for this shit, though?"

"Yeah, I'm ready. So, what I gotta do? Just go and pick up some guns and shit? That's it?"

"Nah. I mean, yeah, but you're going with Malley. She needs you to take her over there."

"Ok. You not coming?"

"Nah. I kinda fucked some shit up with these niggas a little while ago, so I don't need to show my face over there."

"Aight, I feel you. Well, shit, when are we going?"

Block still hadn't called me back with the details about everything yet, so right now we were just playing the waiting game. I told him I needed a few pistols, and at least one chopper in case shit got heavy. I knew he was good for it, but right now, it was just a matter of waiting for him to call me back. In the meantime, we had to keep everything we did on the low. They wanted to smoke, so I told them to go out to the back of the garage. As much as I did my own thing, I still felt like I needed to respect Big Mama's house when I was here. Smoking or drinking in her house wasn't going to happen, and I made sure to keep it as pure as I could in here. I didn't even fuck around with Malley while she was here. She didn't understand it, but she respected it for the time being.

Moments later, they went outside to the back to blow a little bit, but I stayed inside. I wanted to make sure my mind was clear whenever the move had to be made. The weed affected me much differently than it did Quandra and Malley. They could still operate normally under the influence but not for me; I turned into a freaky ass bitch with a slow reaction to everything. There was no way I could fuck with that right now if I wanted to make sure I stayed alive. I leaned back on the couch and propped my feet on the table. I smiled when my imagination put Big Mama in the front room. She threatened to "slap me upside the head," if I didn't take my feet off the table. I laughed but oddly, I removed my feet like she was actually standing right there. I glanced outside once more to make sure everything was ok, and moments later, I laid my head on the pillow and fell asleep.

"Look at this girl here, Mama. Look at her."

I opened my eyes as Mama stood in front of me with her arms folded across her chest, "Lyric, what are you even doing right now?"

"Huh?"

"You heard me. What are you doing?"

"Well, I was sleeping until you came in here waking me up."

She laughed and sat down next to me on the sofa, "Girl, you know you got that smart mouth honestly. I close my eyes, and I swear I think I'm talking to myself. But what are you doing here? Seriously?" I sat up on the couch, "I'm making sure Prince is safe." She shook her head.

"You know, you can make sure he is safe by keeping him out of Milwaukee. You don't need to be here."

"No, I need to be here."

There was a brief pause between us before she spoke up again,

"Well? I'm waiting to hear your lame reason as to why you need to be here because it's not making sense to me."

"Look, I need to make sure he is gone for good. I don't want him popping back up unexpectedly later on. I don't want that kind of trouble, you know what I'm sayin'? I'd rather get rid of it right now when I have the chance."

"That's bullshit, Lyric."

I looked at her curiously, "You can cuss?"

"Lyric, I'm grown, I can do what I want. But, in the same breath, I know you can do what you want just as well. I just don't want you to make the same dumb mistakes I did that cut my life short."

"My life is already cut short."

I got up and walked over to the window and glanced outside. Everything was pure white. The trees, the grass and everything else. It looked as if God himself coated everything in powder and suddenly, I felt a hand on my shoulder. "Honey, if you have faith, the Good Lord can heal you. All you have to do is have faith." I spun around as Big Mama stood in front of me, her gray eyes sparkling as if they were diamonds. She continued, "I know you think it is over, but it's not. The Lord didn't heal me, but it wasn't in his will. My job on Earth was done, and it was time for me to go home, but you? He is not done with you. As a matter of fact, he has not even begun his work with you. You have to exhibit patience, Lyric. Don't rush this and more importantly, don't make any more dumb mistakes because even though you think you are doing Prince well, you will actually be crippling him in his life in more ways than you think." I glared at her as if I was trying to see the whole world in her eyes. For some reason, I couldn't understand what she was telling me.

"What do you mean I will be crippling him? I'm helping him, Big mama."

"You think you are, Lyric, but we all know there is a way that seems right that ends in death."

She started to fade away as I beckoned for her to stay. There was so much more to talk about, but her appearance rapidly faded, and her voice was replaced by a telephone ring. I opened my eyes as my phone rang on the table in front of me. With a raspy voice, I answered,

"Hello?"

"Aight. Everything is set. You can come through now. His name is Garcia."

"Garcia? Aight. I'ma send my girls over there now. Will they be safe?"

"Yeah. I mean, they know how to handle themselves, right? The nigga is a little tricky sometimes but for the most part he shouldn't fuck with them."

I took a deep breath. I didn't want to put them in any unnecessary danger, but at the same time, getting rid of Nas was so engraved in my mind that I couldn't think of anything else. I think Mama was right; I wasn't just doing this for Prince anymore. I mean, I wanted Prince safe, but I think, more importantly, I wanted him to die by my hands and not through some fucking virus. Just my luck, they would figure out some fucking cure, and he'd have enough money to get it. Fucking Magic Johnson and shit, and I didn't want to take the chance.

"Aight, Block, I appreciate this shit man, for real."

"No doubt. Y'all be careful, aight? Hit me back if you need anything else."

"Aight."

I went out to the back and called the two of them in to let them know that everything was straight, and they could roll out there in a few hours. Their glassy eyed look didn't bother me at all. I had seen Malley take shit over when she was as high as a kite, and Quandra was pretty much the same chick when she was high that she was when she wasn't. Honestly, I knew Malley could be trusted, but Quandra still caused me to be on edge. I just never knew with her, and I guess all it took to lose my faith was to get burned one time. I pushed those thoughts out of my head and gave Quandra the directions. "Ok, I know exactly where this shit is at. You want us to roll out now?" she asked. I looked just beyond her as my mind painted a picture of Nas dying right in front of me the way I imagined. I kissed him on the lips one last time before I squeezed the trigger and sent the bullet screaming from the barrel right into his forehead. That's all I wanted right now and honestly, that is all I cared about. The thirst for revenge consumed me, and as my heart pumped blood, the adrenaline kicked in.

"Nah," I said, "y'all can roll out later tonight. Shit don't happen this early."

"Cool. Just give us the word and we out."

The night fell on us like blankets, and before I knew it, it was time for them to go. I gave them some last words before they headed out but they looked at me like I was crazy.

"Uh, who you think you are talking to, Lyric? Rookies? We know how to handle ourselves."

"Aight, my bad. Y'all, handle up then."

"We got you."

With that, I checked outside to make sure no cars were looming around the street, and after everything was clear, they got in the car and took off. Oddly, I prayed for them. I don't know what made me do it or anything, but I felt like it was completely ironic. Not only was I praying, but I was praying for their safety when they went to buy guns. It was crazy, kind of like praying over liquor before you drank it or asking God to make sure your weed wasn't laced with anything. I stopped myself when I realized how absurd it was and from that point on, I just hoped that they would get back here safely. I went back to Big Mama's room in complete darkness so there would be no reason to think anybody was in here if somebody was to roll by. As soon as I walked into her room, I didn't feel the peace that I normally did. It was an eerie feeling of emptiness that was now there, and it was so abnormal that I didn't even want to stay in the room anymore. "Big Mama?" I said out loud, looking for an explanation but there was no response. I turned around and went back into the living room, trying to force myself to sleep but it was no use. There was too much going through my mind for me to even think about sleep. I replayed the voicemails that Prince left on my phone. His cute little voice brought a smile to my face, and even though I could barely understand all of his words it meant the world to me when I heard him tell me that he loved me. At that moment, I began questioning if I was even doing the right thing, but now it was much too late to turn around, and I knew that if I didn't kill Nas, I was going to have to fight my way out of Milwaukee whenever I did decide to leave.

It was around 2 am when the doorbell rang. I must've dozed off without even realizing it as I jumped up and ran to the window. They stood outside looking in every direction to make sure nobody was watching them. I quickly went to the door and let them in. "What up, bitch!" Quandra said as she came through the door with two pistols. Malley walked in right behind her with a Chopper, "Lyric, this shit is mine right here. Fuck! I'm in love with this muthafucka right here!" Quandra closed the door behind them as they walked to the sofa and plopped down.

"Them niggas was cool as a bitch," Malley said, "I think it was because they were trying to fuck, though, you feel me? I wasn't goin', though."

"Hell yeah. That nigga Garcia though? He was fine as fuck! Old Puerto Rican pretty boy ass that looks like he should be modeling some shit instead of selling guns. They came off like they were some killers, though, asking why we needed the guns and shit. I just told them to mind their business."

"You went in, Quandra?"

"Uh, yeah. Problem?"

"Malley was the only one that was supposed to go in. I told them one chick."

Malley put her hand up to stop me, "It's cool, Lyric. They came to the car and checked us out first and then they told her to come in, too. I guess they really did think we were all about to fuck, but they had shit twisted from the jump."

"Hell yeah," Quandra said as she started laughing.

Just then, the front door rattled, and we all spun around in that direction. "Did you lock the door, Quandra?" I asked. "Shit!" she said, and just then the door flung open, and there was a barrage of pistols aimed at us. "Nah uh, y'all should probably put them guns back down. Y'all won't get a shot off before y'all gets sprayed. Just chill, aight? We just want to talk." His Spanish accent was thick and as they walked further into the house, I knew it wasn't Nas or anybody he dealt with. These were all SA's, and they were about eight deep. He smiled at us as they all flooded into Big Mama's house. I looked over at Quandra, her facial expression was blank and immediately I knew she was behind this. We paid them for the guns, and she set it up for them to come back for the guns and keep the money.

"You getting a percentage on this shit, Quandra? Huh?"

"What?"

"Bitch, you heard me. You left the door wide open for these niggas to charge up in here and shit."

She glared at me unforgivingly, and I felt the tension rising between us. Malley spoke up, "Aye y'all—" Garcia interrupted her, "Hey, Mama," he said, pointing the gun directly at her, "you moving too quick. Go ahead and sit yo' pretty ass back down on the couch. I would hate to put a hole in your pretty ass face, okay? Please, Mama, have a seat. We will figure all of this out tonight." Her eyes were still fixated on me, and I didn't turn away from her. It was like we jumped out of the frying pan and landed right into a fucking fire. "Lyric. It's good to see you again," Garcia said, stepping closer to me,

"You're still as pretty as I remember you. It's fucked up that you had to come through the spot and fuck up some of the homies, though. That was some bullshit."

I took a deep breath, "I was just trying to get my son, that's all."

"Hey, hey, it's all right, Mama, you know what I'm saying? Those niggas that got killed back at the spot? They weren't shit anyway. If the homies behind me now were in there, your ass would be dead right now. These boys behind me don't play around for shit. They all got bodies on them, you feel me? But I'm not over here for no revenge or no petty ass shit like that. All I wanted to know beforehand was why they needed these guns, but now, since I have seen you, I want to know more about your boyfriend, Mr. Jones."

"My boyfriend? We don't even talk no more."

He laughed, "Y'all don't talk anymore? What, do you think I'm stupid? I'm asking you nicely, Miss Sutton. I mean, you don't want to be rude, do you?"

"I'm bein' for real, Garcia. I don't talk to him anymore."

He put the gun to my head, "Okay, Lyric, now you're making me angry." He chambered a bullet.

"Damn, Garcia. Listen, I been in Rockwall for the past six or seven months. I came back because the nigga was trying to find where I was at so he could kill me, so I came back to take care of him before he could kill me. That's why we got the guns and shit. I don't fuck with that nigga no more and honestly, I want him dead."

He looked over at Quandra and Malley then he lowered his pistol. "You know, I can tell when people are lying to me and... I hate being lied to. But you? I believe you. I believe everything you said, you know and um, I think we can help each other out. You see, Nas is making a lot of money, and he is trying to move in on my territory on the south side, and I ain't having that shit. Not at all, so I need to take care of him myself."

He paced the room for a few moments as he looked at Quandra, "Oh, and this girl," he said, turning back to me, "she is telling the truth, too. She is not here to set you up. Not even close." Quandra didn't take her eyes off of me as he spoke and not for the first time, I misjudged her. Garcia flipped the light switch. "Nah, you can't do that. They keepin' this house under watch to see if I'm back or not," I said. He squinted his eyes at me for a moment before he shut them back off and took a seat on the couch. Two of the guys with him stood by the door, glancing outside every now and again to make sure everything was ok.

"Now," he said, placing his gun on the table, "let's talk about how we are going to do this."

"We? Your help is not needed."

He smiled, "Well, Ma, I have to admit that I love your bravado, you know? I mean, three fine ass women like yourselves going against a pretty ruthless dude with," he looked at our weapons, "two desert eagles and an AK-47." He laughed, "And I would imagine that Nas probably has those same guns in his room alone and many, many more outside of that. But you say you don't need any help? I will tell you that is the pride and nothing less."

"Look, we just wanted the guns, aight? We paid for them, and that's all we needed."

"Now, now, Lyric, don't be rude, okay? Tell me, why don't you want our help?"

"Because I want to be the one that fires the shot into his fucking head."

"Well, let us help you do that, alright? Do you want the glory? Fine, take it. All I want to do is make sure he dies. End of story."

I looked over at Malley as she sat quietly on the couch waiting for my response. In my mind, I knew this would be the best option for us to take. I had to put my feelings aside and look at this on a whole, and knowing that Garcia and his boys were right here, ready and willing to help me carry this shit out was enough for me. "Aight," I said, "let's get this done." I coughed a few hard times as Malley stood up and patted me on the back. "You need some water?" she asked. I waved her off as I caught my breath. "Aye, y'all fools chill for a minute," one of the guys by the door said. I peeked outside as a car crept past the house. "I know that's them," I said as they slowly rolled by. Garcia glanced out the window next to me, "I see. Well, the next time they roll they ass through here, we are going to be ready for them. I got a plan."

Together, we figured that the best way to pull Nas himself out was to get word to him that Prince was here. The chance that he would show up himself was still iffy, but it was better than it turning into an all-out war on his turf.

"Well, that nigga knows I'm somewhere in the city. The first day I got here, I went to Onyx and got shot at. From that day, cars have been sliding up and down this block to check out the crib."

"We are not worried about that, and as a matter a fact, that plays to our advantage. Next time they stop, we will lure them in. Me and the boys will stay in the back just in case, you know what I'm sayin'? No tellin' what he will bring in if he shows up."

"Aight, that's cool. I'll make sure they come in next time."

With that, Garcia and his boys left but not before they tossed us some more ammo for the guns. I was surprised that he was as cool with me as he was. When he found out that it was me, I expected him to pull out and kill me for what I did to the niggas at his crib, but he said they were dispensable. I understood because that is the same way Nas treated his low-level hustlers. He disregarded them like one dollar bills and usually killed them just to make an example to other niggas on the block. He winked at me and just like that they left as fast as they came in. I looked at the girls; Malley was ready, but Quandra was uneasy. "My bad, Quandra. I just thought that—" She cut me off, "It's cool, Lyric. You know what I'm sayin'. I get where you are comin' from and shit, but I don't even wanna go down that road with you. I understand how you get and if you think something is fucked up, you will act on it. A part of me believes that if Garcia didn't take that gun from you, you would've shot first and asked questions later." She was right, though. The way I was feeling at that moment, being crossed again by the same chick, I wouldn't have been able to keep that shit quiet. I woulda rolled on her at that moment. She grabbed her purse and threw the deuces up to Malley, "Yo, I'ma holla at y'all. Be safe tomorrow, aight?"

She peeked outside before she left and with that, she was out the door. I knew that we may have fared better with another set of eyes behind us but I understood why she felt like she had to leave and now that I think about it, it may have been for the best. Even though she proved that she wasn't the same person, it was difficult to believe that since I guess I hadn't really forgiven her for doing me wrong in the past. She closed the door and left us in darkness as an eerie feeling rushed through my body. The time was near.

Chapter 17

  We chilled outside like I used to do with Vinny and Shaunie when we were younger. The breeze blew against my face as the image of the two of them sitting in the same spots they typically occupied when we were out there solidified in my head. I laughed to myself, imagining Vinny saying some stupid ass shit that always made us laugh. He would be as serious as a bitch, too, as if he was high or something.

"Aye, Lyric. Listen. Ok, so we know Pluto was a planet, right?"

"Yeah."

"Ok, so you know that science just recently said it was no longer a planet. They were basically just like, 'Aye Pluto, fuck yo' lil' retarded ass, you're no longer one of us'."

"Vinny, does this story have a fucking point?"

"Shaunie, shut up! I'm getting to it. Now look, you know we exist too, right? But what if one day somebody just says, 'Yo, you no longer exist,' you know what I'm saying? Just because they say it, the shit doesn't mean it's right. Like, 'Lyric, yo ass don't exist no more,' but um, you still sitting right the fuck here."

  Shaunie and I looked at each other trying to figure out where he was going with it. Suddenly, he spoke up, "Man, fuck y'all and fuck science, too! Science doesn't know shit!" I laughed to myself as Malley turned towards me, "What's funny?" I smiled, "Nothing, just thinking about some shit from before, that's all." We waited on the porch for a few hours, hoping to attract Nas's boys if they rode by. As the sun began to go down, I got a text from Garcia that said he was on his way. I let him know to park in the alley just in case they were here. Moments after that, the white Impala slowly turned down our block, and it was like as soon as they caught a glimpse of me on the porch, it sped up. I grabbed Malley, "They're coming. You ready?" She stood up as if she was and the car stopped right in front of us and waited a few moments before they made a move. I put my hands in my pockets, glaring right back at them and suddenly, the passenger's door opened and Loc stepped out. Three men stepped out the back of the car, smiling, "Ayyyye, Lyric! Man, you are hard to catch up with," one of them said as they started walking closer to me.

"I'm here now."

"We see."

They walked up on the porch and glanced to my right, "Who is that?" Loc asked.

"This is my homegirl, Malley. Malley, you know Loc?"

"Nah, I've never met him."

He peered at her as if he was analyzing her body language, then looked back at me. "Aight, Lyric. You should just come with us." I folded my arms across my chest and said,

"I got Prince in there. Where is Nas at? He doesn't want him?"

"Nas ain't here. Let me see Prince, though, if you don't mind."

"He's in the back."

I turned to go inside and Malley followed. "Nah, she can stay here," Loc said, "she can stay out here with these niggas. If anything goes wrong in here, y'all kill her." Malley turned towards me and just that quick, there was a wrench in the plan, but I had to play it off so they wouldn't think something was up.

"If something goes wrong? Ain't nothing goin' wrong in here, Loc, but aight."

"I've known you long enough to know that you plot. That's what you do, and I respect it, but I know I have to stay on my toes with you."

We walked inside the house, and Loc closed the door behind him as I walked to the back. I checked my phone; Garcia had texted me to say he was out back. I let him know the situation and then put my phone back in my pocket. "Lyric, stop bullshitting and come back out here. We both know that you don't have Prince here," Loc said, his deep voice traveling smoothly through the house. I grabbed the two desert eagles and came out to the front. Loc scowled at me, the pistol in his hand was still relaxed as I came out with the barrels pointed right at him. "So, here we are, Loc," I said, creeping towards him, "this don't have nothing to do with you, aight? I just need Nas."

"Lyric, you know it doesn't work like that."

"Fuck that, Loc. I don't know what type of shit y'all got going on, but I need to get to him."

"Lyric."

"Loc, I'm telling you right now, I need to get to Nas. You need to bring him here, aight? I gotta protect Prince. I gotta protect myself, aight? Please."

"Do you think it is that easy?"

"I don't care how easy or hard it is, I need that nigga here, Loc!"

"Shhhh," he said, "don't raise your voice. Them niggas will come in here spraying, and I don't want you hurt."

"Oh, you don't want me hurt, huh? Just like that day you were supposed to take me out of town? You were trying to see where I was headed so you could let Nas know."

"Bullshit."

"What?"

"Bullshit. I left that day because I weighed my options. I could have taken you out of town and risked being tracked there and get both of us killed or I could leave and let you figure shit out on your own. I didn't want you hurt, Lyric. The truth is, I care about you. I know Nas is on some fuck shit right now, but that is the homie, and I'm not in a position to cross him." He sat his gun on the table as mine were still aimed right at him. That was the one thing about him that I admired, even in the face of death, he was never scared. I wished that I could have that mentality but the truth was, death scared the shit out of me and if I could, I would avoid it all together. The thought of leaving this life and going somewhere that nobody alive has ever seen with their own eyes was enough to make me want to stay here forever. I hated the unknown.

"Damn, Loc.Look, I just need to get to him, aight? I need to. This ain't got shit to do with you."

"Lyric, are you ready to die?"

Just then, there was a knock on the front door. "I'll be out in a minute," Loc said, yelling towards the door. He turned back to me, and that is when a bullet pierced through the window and hit him on his side. He grabbed his rib cage and leaned down to pick up his pistol but before he could grab it, four more shots went off and knocked him completely to the ground. I slowly shook my head as my guns shook in the palm of my hands. Suddenly, Garcia and Malley walked through the door. He fired three more shots into Loc and looked at me, "Aye, Lyric, let's go! Rapid Lament, Ma!"

It wasn't until Malley ran over and grabbed my arm that I snapped out of my daze and ran to the front door. Everybody that was with Loc was laid out on the ground and the porch. They didn't have gunshot wounds or anything on them. Malley grabbed my arm again, "Come on, girl! We gotta go!" She pulled me to the back where Garcia and a couple guys were waiting in their cars. We got in and left the scene as the thoughts of Loc replayed in my mind. *He just wanted to help*,I said to myself as we sped away from Big Mama's house. "Why did y'all kill him?!" I yelled to Garcia.

"Mama, chill out, all right? We have to send a message. That nigga didn't show up, and he wasn't going to show up. Now he knows it's real and there is a better chance that he is going to come out of hiding."

"Fuck! He didn't do shit to deserve that!"

"Deserve?" he said disgustedly, "deserve has nothing to do with it. This is the drug game, and they know that once they get involved, they are not guaranteed to make it out alive. This is a part of the game, Lyric."

We sped through the neighborhoods until we got to the south side. I knew the police would be contacting me soon. This would have been the second murder at Big Mama's house in less than a month, and there was no way that they would buy it being a coincidence. This hadn't gone the way I thought it would, and it was time to improvise. I looked at Malley as she sat by the window without uttering a word. I knew what had to be done, "Garcia, I know where this nigga is at. I think we need to get over there now though because shit is probably a little crazy right now with them knowing that a few of his men were killed. It is the perfect time to catch the nigga off guard."

They drove us to his spot on the south side as darkness blanketed the sky above. I nodded in Malley's direction, and she picked up on what I was saying. As long as we had been together, we were able to develop some flawless nonverbal communication. It was like we were one in the same and I didn't have to say a word for her to understand fully what I was trying to say. Garcia walked a few steps ahead of me and just then, I pulled out my gun and aimed it at the back of his head. He stopped, "Mama, what are you doing?" he said as I reached my hand around his waist and snatched his pistol off his hip. "You're not running this shit right now. Your plan was fucked from the jump, aight? I got business I need to handle, and yo' ass is slowin' me down."

Malley slit the driver's throat and slid into his seat. "Come on, let's go!" she yelled. I kept my gun aimed at him as I backed into the passenger's seat. We pulled off from his spot, his homie dead on the street while we drove further away. "We are going to Nas, right?" she asked. "Yeah. We are going straight to him."

Chapter 18

　　We parked at the end of the alley as streetlights flickered on and off above us like they were signaling our path to Nas's crib. Everything looked the same, and if that was the case, I knew exactly where to go to get inside the house. "Follow me," I whispered to Malley as we crept down the alley to the back of the house. The backyard was empty, and I waited to hear the dogs, knowing that they usually came rushing out as soon as the smallest noise was made. I tapped my gun against the fence to lure them out, and suddenly, two of them charged out of the garage and headed straight to the fence. When they got close, they stopped growling and began wagging their tails. "Thank God they remember me," I said to Malley as I unlatched the lock on the fence. They jumped on me until I gave them the sign to calm down. They both sat, wagging their tails and waiting for the next order, but I didn't give them any. We went to the back of the house, and I glanced up at the window to Nas's room. The light was off as was the kitchen lights. *There is no way that nobody is here*, I thought to myself, *no fuckin' way.*

　　The back door was locked, but Malley was a pro with opening shit that didn't need to be opened. She plucked two bobby pins out of her hair and went to work. Moments later, the door popped open as she winked at me. We both took out our pistols and crept into the house like assassins. The back door opened into a living room that was stripped clean with nothing inside of it except a table and a few chairs. The wooden floor boards creaked whenever you stepped in certain spots, and I remembered that minute detail as I directed Malley across the room. We went into the dining area, the place where there was usually the most men around but oddly that room was just as empty. The old drug rooms were clean, and there wasn't a clue that this house had been a heavy drug spot in the past. "Something ain't right," I whispered to Malley as we stood, looking around the room, feeling the eerie emptiness that accompanied it.

We crept up the stairs, still curious as to why there was nobody or nothing here. We got to Nas's room, and the door was unlocked. I took a deep breath and pushed it open just to see that his room was swept clean. "Fuck!" I said out loud, realizing that this was no longer Nas's spot. He moved, and I didn't know how long ago he left. I realized I had made a wrong move as I looked around. The emptiness made me feel as if I was inside of a warehouse. "What now?" Malley said as she went to the window. "I don't know. I don't fuckin' know."

Just then, my phone rang. It was a number that wasn't saved in my contacts, but I answered anyway,

"Hello?"

"Lyric Sutton?"

"Yes."

"This is Detective Spencer. Where are you right now?"

"I'm out. Why?"

"We need you to come down to the station."

"What is this about?"

"We will explain everything once you arrive. Can you come now?"

I paused for a moment, knowing exactly what this was about and dreading every minute, "Aight. I'll be there."

"Lyric," he said sternly, "Please don't make us come look for you because if you do, we will do it with a warrant for your arrest."

"I said I'll be there."

With that, I hung up the phone and let Malley know what was going on. "Now what?" she asked, nervously. I was pissed that Garcia came to the crib and killed everyone, but that was my fault. I agreed to the shit, but I didn't have to. I could've left that night and did my own thing, and now, I wished I did. We drove down to the police station and Malley parked in the lot.

"I don't know how long I'ma be in here," I said to her, "so I don't know if you wanna chill here or what."

"Lyric, I don't have nowhere else to go. I'ma just chill here."

I walked into a building flooding with police officers. They all glared at me as soon I stepped in as if they knew what I was coming in for. One of the officers stepped to me as I stood at the front entrance. She was short and round with blonde hair flowing from under her cap. "Can I help you?" she asked pleasantly. "Yeah, I'm here to see Detective Spencer." She led me through the police station, past the holding cells that kept people with somber faces behind bars. They looked as if they were begging for someone to let them out and I could only hope that I wouldn't be locked up anywhere in here after I spoke with the detective.

She set me down inside of a small room with a flickering light above me. The chair I sat in was uneven and rocked whichever way my body weight shifted to. It was annoying, and the chair itself was uncomfortable, and I knew why it was that way. This was not a room to get comfortable in; this was a room to intimidate and hopefully prod something out of whoever sat in this seat. Moments later, Detective Spencer walked in and flopped a Manilla folder on the table in front of me. He huffed as he sat down in the seat and intensely looked me in the eyes for a few seconds. "Are you going to tell me why I am here or are you just going to stare at me the whole time?" He reached over to the folder and pulled out snapshots. Four men, one dead on the porch, two dead on the lawn and one dead inside the house. When I saw Loc laying in Big Mama's front room, I cringed inside, but I didn't show any emotions. I couldn't because if I did, the string would begin to unravel and nobody likes a snitch. Snitches don't last long at all here in Milwaukee, and that wasn't even in my blood. I hoped Garcia knew that himself.

"Four men, all dead at your place of residence, Lyric. Four. Well, five if you include the young man who was stabbed there a couple weeks back and died at the hospital. That was your friend, wasn't it? Vinny?"

"Yeah."

"So, you're going to tell me that he died, and now these four men have died all in the same house, and you don't know anything about it? Is that what you're going to tell me, Ms. Sutton?"

"No, I'm not going to tell you anything because I wasn't there. I don't know how these people are getting murdered at my Grandmother's house. I—"

He cut me off, "Bullshit, Lyric. Bullshit. Now, Vinny? I can understand that, okay. You were out in, what, Rockwall? That's what you told me last time, and Vinny had gotten stabbed much earlier that day, so, call me a dumb ass, but I believed you then. Now, we have four, count them, FOUR dead bodies at the SAME SPOT and you want me to believe that you don't know shit about it? You expect me to believe that you don't have anything to do with it?"

"I don't want you to believe anything, but I want you to understand that I didn't kill anybody."

"Well, Lyric, here's the thing. I can put you in that house. I have witnesses that said they saw you there earlier today when they were killed. What are you going to say to that?"

I folded my arms over my chest, "I'm going to say that whoever said that is full of shit."

He could have been right, but if this was a game, I wasn't going to tip my hand. I would rather call his bluff and make him prove himself than to admit to something, even if I knew it was true. I had been around this business too long just to get played by some pissed off detective. "You know who did this, and if I had to guess, I would say you did." I laughed, "Well, you don't have to guess because I'm telling you I didn't do it." He reached into the folder and pulled out another sheet of paper and asked, "What is this?" I glanced down at it,

"It's a chopper."

"A chopper. Okay. AK-47, right?"

"If you know it, why are you asking?"

"Because, we found this in your room. Now, you tell me that if you weren't there and Vinny was murdered weeks ago, whose weapon is this?"

"I don't know. As far as I knew, Vinny wasn't doing no shit with guns, but he did tell me people were chilling at the house with him from time to time, so maybe they know. Shit, maybe it is theirs."

"Who's?"

I lowered my eyes at him, "You want me to do your fucking job for you? Am I getting your paycheck too, or nah?"

He stood up and walked out of the room with a head full of steam. I shook my head and leaned over to look at the pictures again. I moved them out the way until I got to Loc. It was fucked up that he had to get killed especially since I knew he always had my back as much as he could in his position. I couldn't show any signs of emotion or anything because I knew they were watching me through the camera in the room. I had to keep it cool and play it off. Moments later, Detective Spencer walked in,

"Alright, come with me."

"Come with you? For what?"

"We are going to hold you overnight for this warrant."

"Warrant? What warrant?"

"Speeding ticket you never paid."

I laughed, "I can't believe this. For real?"

He cuffed me, "Yeah, for real. I know you know more than what you are telling me, and if we can keep you around a little longer to figure shit out, that's what I'm going to do."

He took me and placed me in the holding cell that I passed when I came in. I knew Malley was still waiting outside, so I used my phone call to let her know what was going on. As covertly as she could, she mentioned Quandra and said that she was able to get some information about Nas. She ended up finessing one of his homies earlier tonight, and when she heard what happened, she said she just wanted to pass the information. I could only hope that they didn't find anything else to use against me and keep me locked up. Once Nas was dead, I really wouldn't care what they did to me. I could rest easy knowing that Prince and everyone connected to me was safe.

They let me out the next morning, and Malley was still in the same spot she was when she brought me last night. "You stayed here all night?" I said as I got in the car. "Nah, I went to see what Quandra was talking about. She showed me where that nigga is right now. We rode past some spot on the north side. Here," she handed me the piece of paper with the address on it. I knew exactly where he was at. It was near a playground right in the heart of the inner city, and I used to go there to watch Junie and Vinny play basketball after school. "Yo, you think—" She cut me off, "She said she would help if we needed her to." I was thankful for that because even though I knew the area, I still didn't know as much as I needed to know in order to slide in there. It was 1 pm when we headed back to Big Mama's house. The yellow tape had been removed from the house, and the front room was stained with Loc's blood. I shook my head when we walked through the door as the same stench of blood stained my nostrils as it did when I saw Vinny. "Damn, you just cleaned shit up, and now it's here again."

I walked to Big Mama's room, and it was just as still as it was a few days ago. No peace fell back on me, no tranquility, just an eerie quietness that seemed to become so loud that I couldn't even stand in the room anymore. I left and walked back to the front and suddenly, there was an overwhelming feeling of sadness piercing through my heart. It didn't take a genius to know what was going on inside me, and I couldn't do anything about it. "Lyric? You aight?" I shook my head, "Nah. Let's just go."

We chilled over at Quandra's house until later that night. She let us know what we needed to do because she was able to get some good information from the nigga she was talking to. She didn't rob him because she figured out a way to make men just give her the money and anything else she wanted without using violence. Bitches do it all day long, but I think that we were just obsessed with being in complete control and flaunting pistols to enforce shit we wanted to do.

"So, yeah, the house is pretty fuckin' secure. Like, you're not just going to walk in there and get to him. It's not so much his men; it's the security system. He has some hi-tech shit, and the door is bolted. I don't know how you get him out, but shit, it's damn near impossible to get in."

I sat quietly, thinking about ways to get him outside but I couldn't come up with anything. "Do you know if he ever comes out?" I asked, hoping she would say yes. "Yeah, he comes out but not as much as he used to." I thought for a minute, and then I figured we would smoke him out, "Let's just rob this nigga's stash houses. The money will make this nigga come out if nothing else does." Malley laughed,

"Shit, I'm down with it! You know I am, especially if money is involved. Quandra, you down?"

She shook her head, "I don't know, y'all. That shit sounds like suicide to me."

"Shit, I'm dying anyway, so it doesn't matter to me."

"What? You're dying?" Quandra asked, her eyebrows raised on her forehead.

"Nothing. I meant that if Nas is still out here, I'm going to die anyway. Yo', that's what we're going to do, though. If you wanna roll, Quandra, you can."

She thought to herself for a moment, "Nah, I'ma let y'all bitches handle that shit. I don't want to fuck with it."

"Aight, that's cool."

Quandra knew the seriousness behind it and I did, too but I didn't care. This is what my life brought me to, and I was ready to deal with whatever came next. Now wasn't the time to turn around—this was the only option.

Chapter 19

I remembered where all the stash houses were, and the only thing Nas did differently was switched their locations from time to time. It was around midnight when we got to the first one. It was the same house that Nas hit me for the very first time. We were dressed in all black, scoping out the surroundings for a little while before we made a move. There weren't many people outside, but I didn't know how many were inside. I told Malley to dress up like a prostitute and stroll past them to get their attention. As soon as they lost focus, I would walk into the house and open up to anybody that was in there. This was the first time we'd ever done something like this, so we didn't have a blueprint for it. It was all a learn-as-you-go-type of thing. Malley got out of the car and walked past a few of the young boys that were out on the porch. "Damn! Aye, you are the finest fuckin' whore I saw in my life! I'd pay for that shit!" one of them said as he walked towards her. The other two boys went right after him, and when they were a good distance away, I snuck in through the front door and headed to the back where the money was kept.

As soon as I walked back there I saw two more men, but before they could react, I fired three shots and all of them connected with the two men as they fell backward into the wall. I heard four more shots outside as I ran to grab the money from under the wooden floor board. After I had picked it up, I ran outside, and Malley was nowhere in sight, but the boys that ran to her were all shot in the back, lying face down in the grass. Suddenly, the lights in our car flickered, and I ran to it. She pulled off as soon as I got in the car.

"Did you get it?" she asked as she drove away.

"I got it."

I tossed the money in the back seat, and we drove to a hotel downtown and checked in. For the next week, that was our routine. We robbed houses left and right, shooting and killing anybody in our path. It was crazy how we both seemed to exhibit the ruthlessness of Nas in our pursuit of him. For a moment, it looked like I felt what he did when he was in the middle of everything. The rush felt like heroin shooting through my veins, and I wondered if this is what my mother and Uncle Stew felt when they injected themselves with the poison. Word got back to Nas that Malley and I were the ones robbing him. At first, he didn't bat an eye, but since it kept happening, he was pissed. We kept people alive just so they could tell him that we were the ones doing it. Malley loved the money we brought in, but I wasn't losing focus on what we were doing it for. We would hit random house's so he could never figure out our pattern, but on the last run I told one of the men where we were going next,

"Tell Nas we will be at the house on 13th next. Let that nigga know we will be waiting for him."

Blood spilled from his leg and at this point, people knew that we were coming for blood whenever we showed up. Suddenly, I felt like the queen of the city. I felt like I was at the top based on the fact that every nigga that saw me knew I wasn't playing games. "Nas is going to be at that next house," I told Malley as we were getting ready, "he is going to be the one tonight, so we need to go a little earlier. I want to be there before he shows up, I don't want him to have the upper hand." Malley fixed her makeup as she spoke,

"Look, Lyric. I know I said I was down with you and all this shit, but I kind of don't want this to end. I think robbing these fucking stash houses is where the real money is at, not finessing niggas and getting a little bit of change. I've made more this past week than I did in a whole month of doing that shit."

"Malley, what the fuck? I thought we were both in this shit for the same reason?"

"We were but shit changes. I say we let Nas keep making money, and we keep robbing that nigga's houses."

"He will eventually catch us, Malley. The nigga is not that dumb. The only reason I pushed the gas is because I came here to get this shit done, not live here."

"Lyric, I mean seriously, though, look at this bread," she said, holding up handfuls of one hundred dollar bills as some dropped to the floor. "Why would you want to stop this? This is money. Real money, Lyric. Fuck a vendetta. We can go from city to city doing this shit and bounce before it get too hot."

"Look," I placed two pistols on both sides of my waist, "if that's what you want to do, then go ahead. But me? I'm here to do what the fuck I came to do, nothing more and nothing less. So, I'ma go handle up and if you're rolling with me, then let's go. If not, do you."

I walked to the door and waited for her to make her decision. After a few seconds, she spoke up, "Go ahead. I'm chillin'." I shook my head and slammed the hotel door behind me. If I was going to do this alone, then so be it. It didn't matter to me because if I was the queen of the fucking city, then I was going to be the queen on my own. Nas wasn't going to make it out of this night alive even if I had to die in the process.

Chapter 20

The neighborhood was empty when I got there. It wasn't that late in the day when I showed up, and I knew what schedule Nas kept his people on. Some things you just don't forget about, no matter how long you've been away. I parked my car a few blocks down and walked the city blocks down to the house. The sidewalks were scattered with fiends and pushers looking to sell or make a quick buck to get their fixes in. I walked past an alley where an older woman was giving head to another dude by some trash cans. It would have jarred me if it wasn't something I was used to seeing, but here in the gutters of Milwaukee that shit was a normal occurrence. If they didn't have the money to buy something, they were always willing to give up anything else for it. Images of my mother flashed in and out of my mind, but I quickly blocked them out. It was something that I didn't even want to imagine her doing, not even in the slightest.

From the time I got to the back door, it was just a waiting game. I sat down, passing the time by scrolling through pictures on my phone of family members and friends. It felt as if not long ago, everybody was still alive and well. The picture of Big Mama, Junie, and Vinny was my favorite. They stood, one on each side of her, like they were her sons. I couldn't even imagine how things would have been for us right now if he was still alive. Would we be doing shows in LA or New York as we thought or would we just be some average entertainers with local fame? Just then, I heard the front door open up and footsteps entered soon after. I shoved my phone into my pocket and peeked through the back window. The window went straight into a room where all the money was kept. I propped the window open and waited for somebody to come in. Moments later, Nas showed up. He was a little slimmer than he was the last time I saw him but for the most part, he looked the same. He went to the area that we used to keep the money and, as he wasn't looking, I hopped in unnoticed. He was bent over, reaching inside a hole in the wall that was covered up with a painting. Before I could get to him, the barrel of a gun was pressed into the back of my head. "Lyric," Nas said without turning around, "I'm glad you made it. Have a seat."

The guy behind me took the gun out of my hand and pushed me against the wall. When I spun around, I saw it was Man-Man. "What's wrong, Lyric? Don't you know how to speak to an old friend? Man-man was yo' nigga at one point, wasn't he? You don't want to say nothing to him?" I remained silent as Nas pulled money out of the bag and began counting it. "Yo, you remember when we used to do this, baby? Just going from house to house collecting thousands and thousands of dollars and then giving you some money to go shopping to get whatever you wanted. Damn," he said, smiling to himself, "those were the good days. You know, the time before you started flippin' out and all that. Up until then, shit was going good, don't you think?" I kept my lock-lipped glare shining on my face. I knew I was going to get caught up. I went in stupidly, not even thinking about him having other guys with him or anything. Things like this happen when you jump the gun, and it was completely out of character for me, but it is what it is.

"Baby, you don't want to talk? I mean, you and that other bitch were running around here, stealing my money and shit trying to draw me out. Now that I'm out, you don't have shit to say? Come on now, talk to yo' man. What's up?"

He put the money back in the bag and tossed it to Man-Man's feet as he stood there with his pistol steadily on me. Nas looked at him and smiled, "Go ahead and talk a walk, fam. I got this." Man-Man grabbed the sack and walked out of the room as Nas shut the door behind him. "Now," he said, glaring directly at me, "we're alone. You got some shit you need to get off your chest?"

"You poisoned me."

"Poisoned you?"

"Did I stutter?"

He rubbed his hands onto his chin,

"Oh, you talking about the HIV shit? Well, yeah, I kinda got that when I was in jail and shit. You know how that go, niggas be in for a minute, and the only thing to do in there to get off is to fuck a nigga that thinks he's a bitch. Well, I fucked a nigga who had the germ, and since we were at odds, I fucked you when you came in. I mean, I feel you though because the nigga that gave it to me? He died as soon as I found out I had it, so you? I completely understand why you're pissed."

When he spoke, I thought back to Malley. She said she had the virus, but if he just got it in jail, then it didn't make sense for her to say she had gotten it from him. One of them was lying, and if I had to guess, it wouldn't be her.

"Bullshit."

"Excuse me."

"You had that shit for a minute, don't fucking lie to me."

"Nah. I mean, one thing about me is I don't mind admitting when I fucked up or did some dirty shit. I'm man enough to say it, but this is not some shit I've had for a long ass time. Shit, don't you die from that shit after long?"

"Whatever."

"Does Prince have it?"

"Fuck you."

"Bitch, does Prince have it? Dumb ass. If Prince doesn't have it but we both had it back then, then he would have it, too."

I thought about that for a minute, and he was right. Even the counselors were shocked when his tests came back negative and what he was telling me was starting to make more sense. *But what the fuck is up with Malley then?* I thought to myself.

"Does Prince have it?!"

"Nah."

"Aight then. But how is Prince doing anyway? You know, it's fucked up that you're keeping my son from me."

"You wanted us dead anyway."

He laughed, "Shit, I did? Well, honestly, I just wanted you dead. I was going to send Prince out of the city, but you? Your hard-headed ass was the reason he got kidnapped anyway. If you would have left like I told you to, then none of this shit would've happened."

"Listen, I didn't come here for no counseling session, aight?"

"Right. You… you came to kill me. Really?" He laughed at the thought of it. "Kill me then, Lyric. I'm here; you're there. Just fuckin' kill me and get it over with. Oh wait, my bad, your dumb ass doesn't even have a gun anymore. What a fuckin' joke. That HIV got yo' fuckin' brains fried up and shit."

Just then, there was a knock on the door, and he smiled, "Right on time. I love a bitch that is right on time! Come in." The door opened, and she walked into the room, her red hair was bright like the end of a match. She switched back and forth on her way over to Nas. "Are you fuckin' kiddin' me?" I couldn't stop myself from saying. Malley walked past me and stood next to Nas as he laughed out loud, "And THIS is how you play the game. THIS is why I am the fucking king of this city, and you are a bottom bitch. Do you think I didn't know? I mean, all the money y'all stole over this last week went back to me. Well, the cut she took went back to me, but for obvious reasons I couldn't get yours."

"Malley? What the fuck!"

"What you mean, bitch? Look, I told you, me and Nas used to talk and when I found out you knew him and used to fuck with him? AND had a kid with him on top of all that? It pissed me the fuck off, but I knew you would lead me back to him, and this nigga here," she leaned over and kissed him on the lips, "this was my first love and you know what they say about first loves, don't you? If they come back to you, then it was meant to be."

"Except if your name is Junie," Nas said as he laughed out loud again.

"Fuck both of y'all. Fuck both of y'all!" I said as I stood up.

Malley pulled out her pistol, the desert eagle I bought with my money, and aimed it right back into my face. "You might wanna calm your little sick ass down," she pretended to cough. "I don't know how you didn't put that shit together. How the fuck am I gonna get HIV from this nigga, he gives it to you, and on top of all that, Prince doesn't have it? Come on now, Lyric! Quandra spoke so highly of you, too. I wanted to see how smart you were for myself, and I must say, I am fucking disappointed! Fucking disappointed!"

I clenched my fists together and lowered my head. So, this is how it was going to end for me. Dead inside of a drug house just like my Uncle Stew. Gone too soon just like my Mother. I couldn't come to grips with it, and suddenly, tears fell out of my eyes.

"This bitch crying?" Malley said, "damn!"

"Well? I guess this shit is over. Bow to the king and queen, bitch."

Nas raised Malley's gun and pointed it in my direction. For a split second, I heard every warning Big Mama sent to me. Her voice pierced through my heart like lightning pierces through clouds in the middle of a rainstorm. Prince grew from a one-year-old to fully grown in the twinkle of an eye. He made it to college and got his bachelor's in sports medicine. He wasn't the best basketball player, but he knew how to help others perform to their highest potential. Stacey remarried, and Serena finally had a few children of her own for Stacey and her new husband to spoil. Life was good, and everybody ended up all right without me around, and as long as I had that glimpse of them before I died, that was all that mattered. Four shots rang out of the pistols and darkness swept over me faster than anything I'd ever experienced before.

I immediately fell to the ground once I felt the shot pierce through my side. The other three shots were fired, and none of them hit me, but moments later, a door slammed open and more shots were fired. I put my hand on my side, and I hadn't felt anything this excruciating since childbirth. More shots rang out in the front of the house as I laid on the ground. My eyes focused in front of me, and I saw it as clear as day, Nas and Malley both laid out on the ground with blood pouring from their bodies. Momentarily, my mind was clear of the pain as I tried to put together what the fuck was going on around me. Just then, I felt someone pull on my arm, "Come on, Lyric! Get up!" More footsteps ran inside the room and looked over at Nas and Malley's dead bodies. "Lyric," Quandra said, "this one is for you." With that, she unloaded the rest of her clip right into Nas's head, and I was scooped up from the ground by the person that was behind me. "Come on, Block," she said, "Let's go!" He brought me out of the house and put me in their truck and moments later, I blacked out.

"Lyric, it's time now, sweetheart. The Good Lord has seen fit for you to have a chance to repent, even in the condition you are in now. If the thieves that were crucified with our Lord had an opportunity to repent on their death beds, then it is possible for you to get the same opportunity."

Big Mama sat on a chair in the hospital in all white while doctors moved around me anxiously.

"Lyric, Baby? You hear me? Now is not the time to delay anything. You have done much wrong in your life, but the blood of the Lord is enough to change everything. Just repent, Lyric. Just repent."

"Lord, I'm…"

I blacked out again before I could finish what I was saying. The next time I woke up, Stacey, Serena, and Prince were in the hospital room. I could hear everything they said, but I was barely able to open my eyes. "Hey Mama," Prince said as clear as day. He looked much older this time around, and I couldn't understand what was going on. Stacey put her arm around him, "Hey, Lyric. We just wanted to stop by and say hi. We know that you can't really talk back to us, but we are praying for your recovery, ok? Doctors say the one bullet pierced through a lot of your organs at once, and it's going to be a while before they know how things are going to go for you." Serena walked up to the bed, and her stomach extended just a bit from her waist. It seemed as if she was pregnant. "Hey Lyric. I miss you, girl, okay? Please come back to us. It won't be the same if you don't." I glared at Prince as he walked closer to me. While he leaned in to kiss me on my cheek, I saw the struggle in his eyes. The eternal battle that seemed to wage between me and Nas took place inside of his soul—the fight to see which one of us he would emulate the most, but honestly, I didn't want him to copy either of us. It pained me to think that he would go through anything me or Nas did in our lives. Nobody wants their child to copy their mistakes, but now, I felt the pain my mother did when she came to me in my dreams to urge me not to be who she was or wanted to be. I didn't know what Big Mama did in her younger days, but I knew she was always trying to keep me on the right path. -He pressed his lips against my cheek, and I closed my eyes.

Chapter 21

I had to learn how to walk and everything all over again. The doctors said I slipped into a coma ten years ago, and when I woke up everything was different. They told me that Stacey came in and took care of me, cutting my hair and making sure my fingernails were trimmed. The most recent time she came in, she told me that Prince was on the verge of becoming out of control. She became his legal guardian when I went into the coma, and she did the best she could, but she was getting older, and Serena moved away after she had gotten married. "I tried my best to keep tabs on him, but that boy does what he wants. He is nothing like Junie was," Stacey said, clearly discouraged with how he was turning out. "That is because he is not Junie, Mom. No matter how much you want him to be, that is not his son. That is Nas's son, and he is going to act just like his father."

I sighed at the thought, knowing that if he was just half of what Nas was it was already trouble. He hadn't stopped into the hospital since I'd awakened from the coma. Stacey said that he told her, "I'll see her when I see her." She also said that word on the streett was that I killed Nas or had something to do with it. If that is what was going around, then I'm sure he heard it by now. It took a few months for me to get my strength back and walk again. It was unbelievable to me how my body kept working when nothing else was. Something kept ticking, and I knew there was a reason behind it. I felt like I had a second chance at life and I didn't want to blow it. Maybe the only way to keep me alive was to put me to sleep for that amount of time. The doctor's told me that the HIV that was in my body had somehow disappeared. They said they can't even explain it but when I went in, I was positive, and after I woke up from the coma, they tested me again, and it was gone. I'm didn't even question it though because I couldn't care less how it happened, I was just happy that it did.

I asked Stacey to drive me past Big Mama's house. She tried to talk me out of it, but I wasn't trying to hear it at all. I wanted to see what happened to her house in the last ten years. The neighborhood was in absolute shambles, and it was surprising that it all happened in so little time. Houses on each side of the block were boarded up, and when we got to Big Mama's, hers was no different. I stepped outside to get a better look at it. The grass was out of control, and the bushes were gone. At some point, they were chopped down from in front of the porch. When I walked up the stairs, grass grew in the middle of the cracks of the steps and the porch itself felt as if it was going to fall apart if I put too much weight on it. The front door was boarded up, and I put the palm of my hand against it as if I was trying to feel its heartbeat but there was nothing there. I glanced at the area me, Vinny, and Shaunie used to sit after school. Suddenly, I remembered how Vinny died, and it brought tears to my eyes. I imagined us both being in our mid-thirties with families of our own. That was something I thought would be reality right now, but things never turn out the way you think they should go. I wiped a tear from my eye as Stacey called out to me, "Lyric? You alright?" I cleared the tears out of my throat, "Yes, I'm good."

I used my cane to help walk down the stairs and back into the car. "You sure you're alright?" she said, looking directly at me. I took a deep breath, "Yeah, I'll be all right, Mama. Let's go." We drove to her home out in Mequon, a suburb of Milwaukee. Her house was huge. "Mama, what are you doing for a living?" She smiled, "Well, let's just say I know how to invest. You know, let my money make money. Allen had written a book before he passed away about tips in the stock business and things of that nature. Well, I got that book published and took the advice myself, and it became a best-seller." It was a two-story house with a big ass front yard and a fence that stretched around the property.

"It's just you that lives here?" I asked.

"Yeah, just me but Serena usually comes up here with her kids on the weekend."

"Kids?"

"Yeah. That girl has two kids now."

"Wow."

"Yeah. They'll be here this weekend, and you'll be able to meet them all."

"Cool. I would love to do that."

She got out of the car, and I tried to get out before she had to come over and help me like I did when we stopped at Big Mama's house. I was almost out by the time she got there, "Girl, you are going to have to stop trying to do all this on your own. Let your strength build up first, okay? There is nothing wrong with a little help." I sighed, "Yeah, I hear you. Is Prince in here?" She shook her head, "he should be, but you never know with that boy. He is just...I don't know, Lyric. Maybe you can help him because I'm about ready to let him stay in Juvie next time."

We walked through the front room and went straight into the kitchen to find Prince looking into the refrigerator with his pants sagging below his ass and headphones over his ears. Stacey came and pulled one side of his headphones up, then let it fall back down and smack him in his head. "Mama, chill!" he yelled as he spun around. That's when I saw him. He was 100% Nas, from facial expressions to attitude. I saw the blank look on his face as he glared at me. Moments later, he nodded, "Whassup Lyric," and put his headphones back on as he continued looking through the refrigerator. Stacey pulled his earphones off and smacked him again,

"What I tell you about calling her that!? That is your mother, and you will call her that!"

"I think I'ma call her whatever I feel like calling her. Thanks, though."

He grabbed a soda and went upstairs. Stacey started to go after him, but I stopped her, "Nah, leave him alone, Mama. I'll take care of it." It took me a little while, but I made my way up the stairs into his room. I twisted the handle and walked in as his back was turned to me and his earphones blasting loud enough to be heard from the door. I walked over to him and snatched them completely off his head. "Mama! Why you keep bugging me!?" he said as he spun around to me. His eyes lowered, and he reached for the headphones that I took from him. "Can I get my stuff back?" he said with an attitude. I gripped them in my hand tight enough to crush them, but I relaxed and focused my attention on him,

"Have you lost your mind?"

"What?"

"I don't know who you think you are, but I know this for sure, you will respect me while I'm here."

"Oh, what?"

"You think you're hard or something? Don't let these little boys you are running around here with getting you in some stuff you can't handle. You must not know what type of chick I was back in the day."

"You was the kind of chick to kill my father, that's what kind of chick you were. I'm living in his name and for him. The streets told me who he was."

"The streets told you half the story then, Prince."

"Yeah, okay. Everybody is telling me half the story. My pop was a street legend, and you couldn't take it because he chose another chick over you and you had to kill him for it?"

"What? Look—"

I felt myself getting angry beyond belief, but I knew that this was my son standing in front of me. I didn't want to hurt him or do anything to him that would damage our relationship more than what it was already. He had something against me and right now, neither of us was in the right frame of mind to talk about it. I swallowed my pride and handed his headphones back to him then walked out of the room. "Close my door behind you," he said as I headed out. I saw every bit of Nas's attitude and my hard-headed mentality inside of him. It seemed as if he had gotten the worse traits of both of us. When I got downstairs, Stacey was in the kitchen cooking dinner.

"What I tell you, Lyric? That boy is something else. I don't know what's going to happen with him."

"Just let me get my strength up. I'll take care of him."

The doorbell rang just as I sat down on the couch. Stacey walked to the front door and with a smile, she let the guest in. "What's up, girl?" Quandra said with a bouquet of flowers in her hand. "Oh my God, Quandra!" I said out loud as she walked over to me. She put her arms around me and kissed me on my cheek, "Damn, girl! I didn't think you were ever going to wake up! I'm glad you did, though, and you still look good! I mean, you lost a little weight or whatever but you still cute in the face." She sat the flowers on the table and Stacey picked them right up to place them inside of a vase. "I came to the hospital to see yo' ass a few times, but you were still out cold. I kept hope, though, you know? I didn't want to see you die."

As she spoke, my mind replayed the last night before I was rushed to the hospital. "Quandra, what happened that night?" She sat back on the couch and smiled, "I was waiting for you to ask that." She went over the scene, step by step. "It was something up with that chick Malley. I mean, she was so fixated on getting to Milwaukee and getting back in touch with Nas. I noticed it, but you know, this was around the time you were still iffy with me, so I didn't even want to bring that shit to your attention." She went on and described how she knew that we were robbing a stash house. "Malley told me that y'all were robbing them houses, but she didn't want to go on the last run because she liked the money too much. That shit didn't make sense to me, though, like, stuff just wasn't adding up. So, Block said you weren't calling him back and he called Shaunie and Shaunie, in turn, called me and put me in touch with Block and that's when I told him the deal. Luckily, his ass was already out here, so it wasn't shit to move in, especially since I knew they weren't expecting either of us."

Out of every person I thought would be the one to come through and have my back, Quandra was the very last person I expected to see. All the times I accused her of dumb shit and she was still right there for me. She either completely changed or what she did to me back in Chicago was a complete mistake. Either way, Quandra was there for me, and I knew she had my back, regardless of anything else that may happen in the future.

"Thank you, Quandra. Even through all the bullshit, thank you."

"Shit, girl, it's all good. Honestly, I didn't like that bitch anyway. For real. I was kind of hoping you would come through and move her out that spot she was in when we were doing that Rockwall shit."

"Yeah, I feel you. How is Shaunie though? She still around?"

"She moved to Cali like two weeks before you got shot."

"Right, I remember that now."

"Yeah. I haven't heard from her since that night she got me in touch with Block. You know we weren't that cool."

"What about Block?"

"Nigga still in Atlanta doing his thang. He does security for the Atlanta Falcons now."

"Big time."

"Hell yeah, he thinks he flies and shit."

She spent a while over there with me as Stacey brought our food out from the kitchen. Fried chicken, macaroni and cheese, greens, and jiffy mix cornbread. "Stacey, girl, if you are cooking like this on a regular, I'ma have to move back here!" I paused,

"Move back?"

"Yeah. I live in Chicago now. It got too hot for me in Milwaukee after, um, after you got shot. I mean, it was just a bad time, and I didn't feel safe, you know?"

I could tell she was speaking in codes since Stacey was around but she laughed, "Girl, look. I don't care what you did or what you had to do for Lyric, all right? I know I'm old, but I'm not slow!" Quandra laughed at her, and moments later, Stacey prayed over the food.

"Dear Father, I want to thank you for bringing Lyric home safely and for keeping her body functioning while she was under your care. I pray that we become tighter as a family and help us to love each other as you loved us. Thank you for this food, and I pray for those who are less fortunate, that you would send them help today in any way, shape or form. In Jesus' name, Amen."

Just then, Prince came down the stairs with his book bag on. We all looked in his direction as he rapped out loud, searching through the closet, "Suzie bedrock the Mic, flow dirty like flint stone toes, su-Suzie rock the mic." I thought I heard things, and I paused just so I could listen closer, "I am the master of this ink penitentiary, words strong enough to wake the dead from the cemetery with my vernacular artillery, you silly if you think you can keep up with the king." I put my plate down and walked over to the closet as he finally pulled his jacket out. This time, I didn't touch his headphones, and he turned around to look me in my eyes. His face was Nas's, but I saw parts of my soul in Big Mama's gray eyes, "Yeah?" he said, removing his earphones.

"Suzie Rock, huh? What you know about her?"

"She was dope from what I heard. I was just listening to a mixtape with some of her songs on there."

"Suzie Rock? You know her real name?"

"Nah, why?"

I smiled and turned to Quandra, "Aye, Quan, Prince said he don't know Suzie Rocks' real name."

"Whaaaat?" she said, laughing out loud.

Prince looked between us just as confused as he could've ever been. "What's so funny?" he asked. "Boy, Suzie Rock is yo' mama!" Quandra said with glee. He wrinkled his eyebrows, "Yeah right. I don't believe that." Just then, I spit a verse from one of my first songs and edited out the curse words.

"Suzy bedrock the mic/flow dirty like flint stone toes/dope lines out my mouth niggas get high when they hear me like they blowin' dro/cats hear me rap, and they swear I ain't write it/so I commit suicide and tell them I'm the ghostwriter."

He stood, his mouth hung open as if he seen a ghost. "I told you," Quandra yelled out from her seat as she stuffed her mouth with macaroni. Maybe this would be the way I could get to him. I could use rap to get his attention and build from there. I know I hadn't been the mother he needed, and it was strictly because I made dumb choices in my life that kept me away from him, but if I was going to make up for lost time, I had to start somewhere. Prince was fifteen now and a freshman in high school so I had to do everything I could to keep him from going down the path I went down. I laughed because it was at that moment that I felt like I was turning into Big Mama.

"Yo mama can flow a little bit," I said as he stood in front of me motionless.

"Man, Suzie was like my favorite rapper, no lie. Do... do you remember any more of your verses?"

"Do I remember? Some stuff you never forget, and I definitely remember my verses."

He looked over at Stacey and then back towards me as he removed his coat and hung it back in the closet. "Mama," he said, "is there some food for me in there?" Stacey took a drink of water and then answered him, "Boy, go in there and get you a plate and stop acting crazy." He smiled at me and then walked past Stacey and Quandra into the kitchen. I took my seat back on the couch next to them, "I got him," I said as I winked at both of them. Big Mama had her way of steering me clear of danger, and it worked to an extent but what used to work for her doesn't mean it was going to work for me. If I was going to reach Prince and keep him on the path I went down, I would have to do it my way and my way was purely through rap. I would have never guessed that my life would end up this way. That Quandra, of all people, would be the one out of all my friends to hold me down to the end. Stacey ended up being the mother that I never had, and the bridge between me and the future would be Prince Nasir Jones. This life was wild, and as I sat with my family, eating, I just had to stop and thank God for replacing what he took away. I lost Junie, Big Mama, Mama, and Vinny but in return, I got Stacey, Quandra, Prince, and Serena, not to mention the little ones she gave birth to that I hadn't met yet. It could have turned out a lot worse than what it did, but I was just grateful that, even in my stubbornness, I still had a chance. After all the failures, I was still breathing, and that was the only thing I needed to keep going. Prince came and sat down on the floor, "Aight, Mama, after this, you wanna battle? I got bars, and I know I can eat you up like I'm about to do this plate right in front of me." I laughed, "Boy, please. Your arms are too short to box with the god."

CPSIA information can be obtained
at www.ICGtesting.com
Printed in the USA
LVHW081054270119
605363LV00059B/579/P